"A brilliant debut...

In just a few minutes, he'd be a married man.

A smile touched Kenny's lips as his six-year-old daughter came down the aisle, tossing flower petals with gusto.

When the bride-to-be entered, Kenny didn't think his lips would move. Wendy's "aunt" Patsy—Kenny's best friend, his lifelong buddy, the woman marrying him to give his daughter a mother—was gorgeous. More than beautiful. She was a vision of life and loveliness.

Patsy's pale pink-and-white gown outlined her every curve. And Kenny's pulse quickened. His knees went weak.

This wasn't the wedding dress of a naive virgin. Or of a self-sacrificing spinster. This was the wedding gown of a sexy, sensuous woman.

His woman. Soon to be...his wife!

Dear Reader,

Happy Valentine's Day! Love is in the air, and Special Edition has plenty of little cupids to help matchmake! There are family stories here, there are breathtaking romances there—you name it, you'll find love in each and every Silhouette Special Edition.

This month we're pleased to welcome new-to-Silhouette author Angela Benson. Her debut book for Special Edition, *A Family Wedding*, is a warm, wonderful tale of friends falling in love...and a darling little girl's dream come true.

We're also proud to present Jane Toombs's dramatic tale, *Nobody's Baby*, our THAT'S MY BABY! title. Jane also has written under the pseudonym Diana Stuart, and this is her first book for Special Edition under her real name. And speaking of firsts, please welcome to Special Edition, veteran Silhouette Desire author Peggy Moreland, by reading *Rugrats and Rawhide*—a tender tale of love for this Valentine's month.

Sherryl Woods returns with a marvelous new series— THE BRIDAL PATH. Don't miss the first book, *A Ranch for Sara*, a rollicking, heartwarming love story. The second and third titles will be available in March and April! And the Valentine's Day thermostat continues to rise with Gina Wilkins's sparkling tale of opposites attracting in *The Father Next Door*.

Finally, Natalie Bishop presents readers with the perfect February title—*Valentine's Child*. This tale of love lost and then rediscovered is full of the Valentine's Day spirit!

I hope you enjoy this book, and each and every title to come!

Sincerely,

Tara Gavin, Senior Editor

Please address questions and book requests to:
Silhouette Reader Service
U.S.: 3010 Walden Ave., P.O. Box 1325, Buffalo, NY 14269
Canadian: P.O. Box 609, Fort Erie, Ont. L2A 5X3

ANGELA BENSON

A FAMILY WEDDING

Published by Silhouette Books
America's Publisher of Contemporary Romance

To Harriet, who said it would happen, and to Monica,
who rejoiced when it did.

 SILHOUETTE BOOKS

ISBN 0-373-24085-6

A FAMILY WEDDING

Copyright © 1997 by Angela D. Benson

This edition published by arrangement with Harlequin Books S.A.

® and TM are trademarks of Harlequin Books S.A., used under license.
Trademarks indicated with ® are registered in the United States Patent
and Trademark Office, the Canadian Trade Marks Office and in other
countries.

Printed in U.S.A.

ANGELA BENSON

When Angela Benson sold her first book in 1993, it was a dream come true. Since then, Angela has continued to dream. And with the publication of *A Family Wedding*, her sixth book and her first category title, she's seeing those dreams come true.

A graduate of Spelman College and Georgia Tech in Atlanta, Angela is a former engineer who now writes full-time while she works on her second graduate degree. She was born and raised in Alabama and currently resides in the Atlanta suburb of Decatur. When she's not weaving her own tales of romance, Angela can be found curled up on her couch reading her favorite romance authors.

Angela loves to hear from readers. Write to her at P.O. Box 360571, Decatur, GA 30036 or send E-mail to abenson@atl.mindspring.com. If you're adventurous, you might want to visit her Home Page at http://www.atl.mindspring.com/~abenson/. She'd love to see you there.

Dear Reader,

I'm honored to join the Silhouette family and the wonderful Special Edition authors who bring you such warmhearted stories each month. I've always been a lover of romance and of Special Edition novels, so being able to share my story with you is a special treat.

A Family Wedding is a story from my heart. Kenny, Patsy and Wendy allowed me to experience love in all its wondrous variations. From the love between a father and daughter to the love between lifelong friends to the warm, spine-tingling love between two people who find that their perfect mate has been right beside them all their lives.

As you welcome the month of February, and with it Black History Month and Valentine's Day, I hope that *A Family Wedding* adds to your celebration and reaffirms the truth that love is a universal language.

Sincerely,

Angela Benson

Chapter One

"God bless Daddy and Aunt Patsy and Grandma Ellis and Grandpa Ellis. And God, please say hi to Mommy and tell her that I love her and miss her. And say hi to Grandma Sanders and Grandpa Sanders, too."

Kenny Sanders listened to his six-year-old daughter, Wendy, as she knelt at the side of her bed. Her words were like a knife in his heart.

Remarkably, Wendy seemed to be handling the deaths of her mother and grandparents much better than he was. She was a happy child. Her face usually held a joyful smile and her eyes twinkled. Kenny thanked God for her every day. He didn't know what he'd do if he lost her, too. He hoped he'd never find out.

"Oh, and God bless my new friend, Mrs. Walden," Wendy was saying. This was the first time Kenny had heard Wendy mention the name. He didn't like her having adult friends he didn't know about, especially with the kooks running around these days.

"Amen," Wendy concluded. She got up from her knees and hopped into the white canopied bed Leah had been determined she'd have. Kenny smiled at the thought.

"Who's Mrs. Walden, Peanut?" Kenny asked.

"She's a new teacher at school. Except she's not really a teacher. She said she was my friend."

Apparently this Mrs. Walden was a teacher's aide, Kenny thought as he tucked the pink-and-white covers around his daughter. He'd make a point of meeting her on his next visit to the school.

He tugged on one of the dark braids covering Wendy's small head. "I'll have to meet this new friend of yours."

Wendy smiled the dimpled smile she'd inherited from him, and her eyes lit up with excitement. "Does that mean you're coming to my class again, Daddy?"

Kenny answered her smile with his own. He'd visited Wendy's class once before, on Career Day. "So you like it when your daddy comes to visit your class?"

Wendy leaned forward and wrapped her short arms around his chest. "I love it when you come to my class, Daddy."

Kenny hugged her small body, glad she was his daughter and glad she loved him as much as he loved her. "And I love you, Peanut," he said, giving Wendy a final squeeze before helping her lie down again. He'd been a parent long enough to know that even though her words were sincere, she wasn't above using them to extend her eight-thirty bedtime a few minutes longer.

"Oh, Daddy, do I have to go to sleep now? I'm not

sleepy." The practiced pout was there, and though it was effective, he wasn't giving in to it tonight.

"Yes, you do, young lady," Kenny answered, his voice full of the warmth and love he felt for her. He tugged at one of her braids again. When he got the smile he wanted, he leaned over and kissed her forehead. "Good night, Peanut."

"Good night, Daddy. Sleep tight and don't let the bedbugs bite."

"We don't have bedbugs, Wendy," he said, performing his role in the nightly ritual. She giggled as he switched off the light and left the room, closing the door behind him.

Kenny trooped down the carpeted stairs of the recently renovated eighty-year-old house he and Wendy shared. Friends had told him he was crazy to move out of the home he and Leah had bought. Wendy needs the continuity, they'd said. But Kenny didn't agree. He and Wendy needed a fresh start. They'd brought most of their furniture with them, so some things were the same. But some things weren't. This house didn't hold the pain the old house had. This house held hope for a new beginning.

Kenny hunkered down at the mahogany desk in the first-floor room he'd designated as his office and pulled the depositions for the Thompson trial out of his briefcase. Being in private practice allowed him to choose his cases, but sometimes he was still forced to work extended hours. He made it a point to hold off on the overtime until after Wendy was asleep. That decision resulted in many long nights, but the uninterrupted time with his daughter was more than worth it.

For the millionth time, Kenny wished he'd listened

when Leah had tried to tell him that over the years. But he hadn't.

Now he understood. Family was important. He wished he and Leah could have shared more nights together with Wendy, watching her grow. But wishing couldn't change the past. The fact was he hadn't been a good husband to his wife until she was too sick to enjoy him. He only hoped she looked down on him now and took joy in seeing that he'd learned what she'd tried so hard to teach him. It wasn't much, but it was all he could hope for.

"Daddy," Wendy said the next morning, her mouth packed with one of the pancakes Kenny had prepared for breakfast.

"Don't talk with your mouth full, Peanut. I've told you about that," Kenny chided. He heaped four pancakes and six strips of bacon on his plate and took a seat at the kitchen table next to his daughter.

"I forgot," Wendy said, her mouth still full.

Kenny hid his smile by taking a swallow of his orange juice. He found that keeping a straight face when his daughter did something funny but not appropriate was one of his toughest parental jobs.

"Daddy," Wendy said again, this time with no food in her mouth. "Do you think God will send me a new mommy?"

Kenny choked on his juice and then patted his chest to get the air flowing in his lungs again.

"Are you all right, Daddy?" Wendy asked, her eyes full of fear. That look was one he'd hoped never to see again. Fear. Fear of the unknown. Fear of losing someone else.

Kenny quickly cleared his throat and reassured his daughter that he was fine.

"So," Wendy repeated, "do you think God will send me a new mommy?"

Kenny looked into the big, brown eyes that were identical to Leah's and stalled for time. "Do you want a new mommy, Peanut?"

Wendy scrunched up her pug nose while she pondered the question, her milk mustache making her look like a circus clown. "Mommy said I would get a new mommy when it was time. Is it time yet, Daddy?"

Kenny felt as if he'd been gut-punched. Leah had said this to Wendy? He gazed out the window at the clear blue morning sky, a hint of the beautiful spring day to come, and tried to come up with an appropriate answer to Wendy's question. He hadn't formed one when he returned his gaze to her.

"What made you think of this now, Wendy?"

She hunched her small shoulders and stabbed her fork into her remaining pancake. "All the other girls at school have mommies. Meg Thomas has two. And Carrie Williams got a new mommy after hers died. I just thought it might be time for God to give me my new mommy."

The matter-of-fact way she answered his question relieved some of his anxiety. It didn't appear that she'd been thinking too long or too hard about the new mommy Leah had promised her. He had some time to work out an answer.

He glanced at his watch. "It's time for school, Peanut. Finish your breakfast so we can get going. We'll talk about your new mommy tonight."

Wendy chattered for the entire drive to the school. Kenny made the appropriate responses, but his thoughts were still on her earlier question. He thought he'd done a good job with Wendy, but obviously she needed more. She needed a mother.

What was he going to do? It wasn't as if he had a spare woman lying around that he could up and marry. Hell, he hadn't even dated in the two years since Leah's death.

When he pulled into the school yard, Wendy leaned over and kissed his jaw. "See you later, Daddy." She opened the door and bounded out. Before she reached the playground, she turned around and yelled, "Don't forget Aunt Patsy is coming over tonight. She said she had a surprise for me."

Kenny should have chastised Wendy for yelling, but the thought of his best friend's visit took over his thoughts. He'd tell Patsy about Wendy's question. Maybe she'd have some insight for him.

From her seat on the overstuffed couch in her living room, Patsy Morgan stared at the envelope propped against the floral centerpiece on her dining-room table. She'd picked it up more than once since she'd gotten it out of the mailbox yesterday, but she had yet to open it. Who would have thought a letter would have this kind of effect on her? she wondered. It was only a letter.

Now that was a lie. It was more than a letter. It was a symbol of the biggest failure in what seemed to her like a lifetime of failures. She knew she was overreacting, but she couldn't stop herself.

She slowly got up from the couch and inched her way to the table. She picked up the crisp, ivory envelope and turned it over in her hands. "Jacobson and Son, Attorneys-at-law," she said, reading the return address. She didn't have to open the envelope to know what was in it. It was her final divorce decree.

Six years of her life wiped away by a single sheet of paper.

She carefully lifted the sealed flap of the envelope, as if honoring the solemnity of the moment. "This document signifies the dissolution of the marriage of Patsy Morgan Baxter and Theodore Randolph Baxter," she read, before the tears in her eyes blurred the rest of the words. She placed the document back in the envelope and laid it on the table before dropping into one of the upholstered dining-room chairs.

Theo had been the love of her life. From the day she'd met him, there had been no question that she'd marry him and bear his children. She laughed dryly. She'd married him all right, but there'd been no children. And for that she was grateful. For a child, there was no such thing as an amicable divorce. She knew that because she still bore the scars from her parents' divorce.

Patsy pushed her unruly mane of black hair away from her face. What had happened to her and Theo? she wondered. She'd loved him so much, and they'd been so full of hope and plans for the future. She remembered clearly the passion they'd shared during their courtship and the first two years of their marriage. It had been all she'd hoped for.

But something had happened. Suddenly their passion was gone. She had known the end was near when she'd found herself studying the patterns on the ceiling while she and Theo made love. Of course, he'd noticed the change in her, in them, but he was no more able to talk to her about his feelings than she was able to talk to him about hers.

When their desire waned, there was nothing left for them. Though she and Theo had shared a passion that was ten degrees above boiling, she now realized they hadn't had the deep, abiding friendship it took to make it through the normalcy of day-to-day life. When the passion fizzled, so did the marriage.

Soon after, Patsy had learned about Leah's illness and understood that her lifelong friend, Kenny, needed her to help with his daughter. It was easy to pack up and move back home to Grove City, Virginia. Theo hadn't tried to force her to stay. He'd known their marriage was over as well as she had.

Surprisingly, in the two-and-a-half years since they'd separated, neither had taken the time to file for divorce. Until now. Theo had found somebody else and Patsy was glad for him. She just hoped he'd learned from their union and had cultivated a relationship that would endure the long haul.

Propping her legs up on the chair nearest her, she rolled her shoulders forward and pulled the belt of her ratty terry-cloth bathrobe tighter around her waist. She'd been smart to call and tell her secretary she wouldn't be in today. She needed the time to adjust to her new marital status. She laughed. "Like my new marital status will make a difference."

She picked up the envelope again. It *was* only a letter, she thought. She turned it over in her hands a couple of times before getting up and heading for her bedroom.

Once there, she got down on her knees and reached under the bed for the metal storage box that held all her private papers. She punched in the combination, opened the box and placed the letter on top of the other important papers in her life. She locked the letter away as she'd locked away her passion many years ago.

Patsy lowered the vanity mirror in her brand-new powder blue BMW and patted her new hairdo. When she'd decided to pamper herself as a way of celebrating—or rather, dealing with—the divorce decree, she'd thought it was just something to do. She hadn't realized she'd be in for a major overhaul. A new hairdo, some new clothes and a makeover were one thing, but a new car—well, she knew that was a bit much.

Satisfied that every strand of her new, short and, hopefully, more manageable hairstyle was still in place, she snapped the vanity mirror closed, picked up the gift box in the passenger seat and opened the car door.

When her new, burgundy leather pumps hit the sidewalk, Patsy felt a wave of exhilaration. She tried to pull her matching leather skirt further down her thighs, but to no avail. It was a short skirt. Pulling on it wouldn't make it any longer.

She wondered what Kenny would think of her new look. Would he even notice? She wasn't sure he would. Most of the time Kenny didn't even think of her as a woman. She was his buddy, as she had been since they were children, living on the same block. Kenny's home had been a refuge for her during her parents' breakup.

She wondered again what he would think of her new look. If he made some wisecrack, she'd smack him. She meant it, too. She'd learned early that when Kenny was in a joking mood, you couldn't reason with him. No, at times like that, he only understood physical reasoning.

Patsy rapped the knocker on the solid oak door, amazed again that Kenny had sold the contemporary house he'd shared with Leah and bought and renovated this old place. Not that she didn't understand what he'd been doing. She did. She was very familiar with running away from pain. She'd done it with Theo. She was doing it today. Why shouldn't Kenny do it with a house?

Her thoughts lightened and a smile crossed her face

when she heard Wendy's high-pitched voice. Patsy had fallen in love with the incorrigible child. Their relationship benefited both of them, Patsy thought. Wendy was the little girl she had always wanted. And Patsy was the friend Wendy needed to help her understand her mother's illness and death.

"Aunt Patsy?" Wendy asked when she opened the door. The wonder in her eyes made Patsy's smile widen.

"Of course it's me, Wendy," she answered. She extended the gift box. "Who else is bringing you gifts today?"

Wendy reached for the wrapped package, but her eyes never left Patsy's face. "You look like a princess, Aunt Patsy. You're so pretty."

Patsy leaned down and kissed Wendy on her forehead. "Thanks, sweetheart," she said, automatically straightening the collar of the little girl's plaid shirt. "But you're the princess. I'm just Aunt Patsy."

Those words cut through Wendy's amazement, and she stepped back so Patsy could enter the house.

"Where's your daddy?" Patsy asked, her eyes roaming the room. Wendy's reaction to her new look made her anxious for Kenny's.

"He's cooking steaks on the grill."

As if he'd heard them talking about him, Kenny chose that moment to make his entrance. He sported faded jeans and a maroon Morehouse sweatshirt that fit him as if custom-made for his muscular six-foot frame.

"Patsy," he said, his deep voice full of mirth. "What's up with you?" He pulled her fully into the foyer. "Turn yourself around so Wendy and I can get the full effect."

Patsy obeyed. She took Wendy's and Kenny's responses to mean she didn't look like a fool. "So you like it?'' she asked, touching her hair, but referring to her new outfit, too.

Kenny smiled down at his daughter before gazing back at Patsy. ''Aunt Patsy is a beauty, isn't she, Wendy?''

Wendy bobbed her head. ''She looks like a fairy princess, Daddy.''

Kenny laughed. Not many princesses he knew dressed in leather miniskirts. ''Maybe the princess will have dinner with us.'' He looked at Patsy. ''I already have a steak on the grill with your name on it.''

''Please, Aunt Patsy,'' Wendy begged, pulling on Patsy's arm. ''Stay for dinner.''

Patsy couldn't resist the pair. This wouldn't be the first time they'd shared a meal. They did it about once a week— sometimes here, sometimes at her house. She squeezed Wendy's hand and lifted her gaze to Kenny, not missing the laughter in his eyes. ''Sure, I'll stay.''

Kenny gave a quick nod, then directed his attention to Wendy. ''So what did Aunt Patsy bring you, Peanut? And did you remember to say thank you?''

Wendy stared at the box in her hand. ''I forgot, Daddy.''

Kenny looked up at Patsy with an expression that said he could believe that. ''Well, now you remember.''

Wendy pulled Patsy after her as she skipped to the family-room couch with her present. She sat down and ripped the box open. Patsy smiled at her impatience.

Wendy lifted the ebony-hued porcelain doll from the box and exclaimed, ''Oh, wow! I love her, Aunt Patsy.'' She reached over and kissed Patsy's cheek. ''Thank you, thank you, thank you.'' Wendy looked up at her father and extended the doll to him. ''Isn't she pretty, Daddy? Just like Aunt Patsy.''

Patsy caught the quick, questioning glance Kenny threw her way before he answered his daughter. "Yes, Peanut," he said. "She is pretty." He glanced at Patsy again, then added, "Just like Aunt Patsy."

Patsy knew from his concerned glance he had guessed there was more to her makeover than a sudden need for a new hairdo. But she also knew he'd wait until Wendy was in bed before he'd ask her about it. In fact, she counted on it. She wanted to discuss her feelings with him. Maybe, with his help, she could finally get some resolution and move forward with her life.

Kenny left Patsy and Wendy oohing and aahing over the doll and went back to the grill on the deck. As he flipped over one of the steaks, he decided he liked Patsy's short hairstyle. She'd often complained that her longer hair was too hard to control. He smiled. Sometimes her head had looked sort of like a bird's nest. But every strand of this new style was in place. The short cut made her look more in control and at the same time more feminine. It gave her a softness and vulnerability that he found most attractive.

And that outfit. Man, was that some outfit! He'd never seen her dressed so...so provocatively before. Thoughts of her long legs extending from the short leather skirt made him wonder why he hadn't noticed them before. He'd been so caught off guard by her new look that he'd almost missed the sadness that threatened to cloud her eyes.

Patsy was his best friend, and he hated to think of her in pain. She'd been there for him when he needed her and he'd be there for her through whatever it was that was making her sad. He just wondered what it was.

It probably had something to do with that jerk she'd

married, he thought. He'd never understood what Patsy had seen in Theo Baxter in the first place. He'd been all flash and no substance. The kind of guy that usually repulsed her. But not that time. There had been something about Theo that had gotten under Patsy's skin quickly and surely.

And just as Kenny had always thought would happen, Patsy had gotten hurt. That hurt had been easy for him to see even in the midst of his own grief.

He and Patsy had talked about the failure of her marriage many times. And those conversations always ended with Patsy saying the intensity of the love she'd shared with Theo had been the downfall of their marriage. In her opinion, their passion had been a crutch that kept them from developing a deeper relationship. When the crutch was gone, the marriage had nothing left to stand on.

He'd tried to convince her that the failure of her marriage had nothing to do with passion in general, but with Theo in specific, but she'd hadn't bought it. Instead, she'd found herself in a tragic catch-22. She feared entering another relationship with that kind of desire because she didn't think it could last. But having *experienced* that kind of passion, she couldn't imagine a fulfilling relationship without it.

Kenny flipped over the last steak. Maybe the new outfit and hairdo meant she was changing her mind. Maybe she'd decided to take his advice and try again. He hoped so. If anybody deserved to be happy, Patsy did. She was a good woman and a good friend.

Thoughts of Patsy and her trying again made Kenny remember Wendy's question. His daughter wanted a new mommy, and God knows he wanted only what was best for her. Could he himself try again? For Wendy's sake?

Chapter Two

"I love my doll, Aunt Patsy," Wendy said. She brushed her hands across the doll's head. "She has braids like me."

"That's why I got her for you. A special doll for a special little girl."

Wendy put her doll down on the coffee table and rubbed one of her hands across Patsy's head. "Your hair is so pretty. I wish my daddy would let me cut my hair. Audrey Simmons got her hair cut."

"Well, you're not Audrey Simmons. You're Wendy Sanders and you don't need your hair cut."

"You cut yours," Wendy reasoned.

Patsy fought back a smile. "Well, I needed a change today."

"I need a change, too."

Patsy laughed at the grown-up tone Wendy used. Sometimes she forgot how tenacious the child could be once her mind was set on something. "Do you want me to redo your braids while your daddy finishes dinner?"

Wendy's eyes twinkled. "Will you, Aunt Patsy? Will you?"

"Sure. Now go get your hair basket."

Patsy watched Wendy scamper out of the room. She braided Wendy's hair about twice a week, and they both enjoyed it. She knew Kenny could braid as well as she could, if not better, and she appreciated that he shared the job with her.

"Here you go, Aunt Patsy." Wendy was back with her hair basket in one hand and her dolls' hair basket in the other.

"Sit." Patsy pointed to the spot on the floor in front of her.

Once Wendy was seated, she picked up her doll from the coffee table and began combing its hair. "Aunt Patsy," she asked, "do you think God will send me a new mommy soon?"

Patsy stopped in the middle of taking down one of Wendy's shoulder-length braids. "Do you want a new mommy, sweetheart?"

Wendy shrugged her shoulders. "All the girls at school have a mommy."

"So you want a mommy so you can be like all the girls at school?"

Wendy bobbed her head. "Do you think a new mommy would let me get my hair cut?"

Patsy smiled in relief. Obviously, Wendy wasn't too torn up about this mother issue. Patsy would be sure to mention the conversation to Kenny, though.

"I think your new mommy would agree with your daddy, Wendy. You aren't going to get your hair cut."

"But, Aunt Patsy—"

Patsy shook her head. Kenny was going to have his hands full with Wendy and her haircutting idea.

When Kenny entered the family room a little while later, Patsy was whispering in Wendy's ear. What she said must have been funny because Wendy smiled. Seeing Patsy and Wendy like this made his heart fill with love. They were the two most important people in his life. In the ways that counted, the three of them were a family.

"Steaks are ready, ladies," he said. They both looked up at him and giggled. "What's going on?" he asked. "Did I say something funny?"

Patsy whispered something else in Wendy's ear and again the little girl smiled. "We can't tell you, Daddy. It's girl talk."

Kenny walked over and stood in front of Wendy. He folded his arms across his chest and looked from her to Patsy and back again. "Girl talk, huh? I bet I can make you tell me." He picked Wendy up and began tickling her. "Now are you gonna tell me?"

Between giggles, Wendy managed to insist, "It's girl talk, Daddy."

He dropped her on the couch and began placing noisy kisses all over her face. Patsy laughed at their playfulness. She loved seeing them like this. This was a family.

"Daddy," Wendy protested, her eyes bright with mischief and tears of laughter. "You didn't tickle Aunt Patsy."

Patsy snaked one of her fingers into the gap between the two bottom buttons of Wendy's shirt and tickled her tummy. "Your daddy knows better than to tickle me. When I was your age, I was the tickling champ. Nobody could make me laugh." She glanced over at Kenny. "Not even your dad."

"I think that's a dare, don't you, Peanut?"

Wendy nodded vigorously.

Kenny's gaze met Patsy's, and she knew he couldn't resist her challenge. "You're going to get it now," he said, leaning toward her. "Come on, Wendy, let's make Aunt Patsy laugh."

Wendy attacked Patsy immediately with fumbling tickles. Her father quickly followed. Patsy couldn't help but laugh. Not because she was ticklish, but because she loved them both so much. "Okay, okay," she said between giggles. "I give up. You can stop now."

Kenny pulled away first, then Wendy.

"We made you laugh, Aunt Patsy. I knew we could do it."

Patsy tickled Wendy one last time and made her giggle. "You sure did."

Wendy was about to launch into another bout of tickling with Patsy, but Kenny pulled her back. "We'll have to tickle Aunt Patsy later. Our steaks are getting cold." He picked Wendy up from the couch and placed her on the floor. "Now go get washed up."

With a smile, Patsy watched Wendy run out of the room. "She's adorable."

"Like me at her age."

Patsy rolled her eyes. "You've got to be kidding. Wendy's adorable. You were an unholy terror."

"Hey," Kenny said, getting up from the couch, "I was a very active child."

"I was there, Kenny. You were an unholy terror."

Kenny glanced toward the stairs, looking for Wendy. When he didn't see her, he asked, "What happened today?"

"I got a makeover," Patsy answered, even though she knew Kenny was talking about more than her new look.

When he didn't smile at her attempted humor, she said, "Let's talk about it later."

He hesitated, then said, "It's about Theo, isn't it?"

Patsy slowly shook her head. Sometimes she and Kenny read each other too well. "Please, Kenny. Let's talk about it later." The concern and caring in his eyes almost unleashed the tears she'd been fighting.

Kenny looked as though he was going to force the issue, but he didn't. He touched her face. "Theo was a fool, Patsy."

Patsy bowed her head and a tear fell from her eyes. Kenny brushed it away with his finger and smiled at her. "We'll talk about it later. Let me go check on the steaks." He touched her cheek again and left the room.

"Anybody want dessert?" Kenny asked after they'd finished their dinner of steaks, baked potatoes and green peas. "I made cheesecake."

"I do, I do," Wendy sang.

"None for me," Patsy said with a smile. She'd enjoyed both the meal and the company, and she was much more in control of her emotions than she'd been earlier.

"I thought you loved Daddy's cheesecake," Wendy said. "He has your favorite strawberries and everything. You have to have some."

"Okay," she agreed for the child's sake, "I'll have a small piece."

"Yeah," Wendy said, clapping her hands together. "Everybody gets cheesecake."

Kenny left the room, but he was back in a flash with the dessert. He cut small slices for Patsy and Wendy and a larger one for himself.

"I want the other piece," Wendy said, her infamous pout in place.

"That's Daddy's piece," Kenny explained, pointing to the larger slice.

Wendy was about to complain, but Kenny gave her a firm look that brooked no more discussion. She stabbed her fork into her smaller slice of cheesecake and put a big piece in her mouth. Patsy smiled when Kenny looked at his daughter as if he could strangle her and Wendy looked back at him with a smile of pure innocence. The father-daughter tug-of-war was in full swing.

"It's good, Kenny," Patsy said after her first bite. As she'd hoped, Kenny turned his attention to her. "You missed your calling. You should've been a chef."

"Cooking is only one of my talents," he boasted.

"More like your only talent," Patsy teased, enjoying the exchange.

Kenny looked over at Wendy. "I think Aunt Patsy needs another tickling. How about you?"

"Yeah, let's tickle Aunt Patsy," Wendy said.

Patsy held up both hands. "Okay, okay, I apologize. Now will you guys forget about tickling?" She turned her attention to Wendy. "What did you do in school today?" she asked.

As usual, Wendy was ready to talk. Patsy kept her eyes focused on the little girl as she was regaled with the happenings at school. She felt Kenny's gaze on her as she and Wendy talked and knew he was wondering if she was okay. It warmed her insides to know he cared.

"You don't have bedbugs, Wendy," Patsy said, flashing a smile in Wendy's direction before turning off the light in the bedroom and closing the door. She thought again how Wendy had captured her heart. She wished, as she often did, that she'd been around when Wendy was an infant. But that hadn't been possible.

As Patsy walked down the stairs to the kitchen, her thoughts turned to Leah. When Leah found out she was dying, she'd called Patsy and given her the news…told her that Wendy and Kenny were going to need her.

The six months before Leah died had been hard for the four of them. For Kenny, because he'd been comforting a dying wife while trying to maintain a relatively stable home for his daughter. For Patsy, because she'd had to watch her best friend suffer through the agony of seeing his wife slowly slip away from him. For Wendy, because she hadn't really understood why her mother was leaving. And mostly for Leah, who'd died a brave death thinking only of her husband and her child.

Patsy was sad that Kenny had lost a wife and Wendy had lost a mother, but she was happy they'd shared Leah's love. Leah had been a wonderful mother and a loving wife. Patsy wondered if Kenny would ever find another woman like her. Now, after two years, she wondered if he would even look for one.

"I didn't hear you come down," Kenny said when he glanced up from his task of putting the dinner dishes in the dishwasher. "Wendy didn't try to make you stay longer?"

"You know she did, the little bugger." Patsy laughed. There was a time when she'd been wrapped around Wendy's finger. Patsy was a quick study, though, and she'd caught on to the little girl's machinations. "But I've learned."

Kenny smiled. "You have, haven't you? You're good with her, Patsy. You'll never know how much I appreciate what you've done for her. For both of us."

"I didn't do any more for you than you would've done for me."

Kenny nodded. Patsy was right. He would do anything

for her. After closing the door to the dishwasher and turning it on, he walked over and took her by the arm. "Let's go sit down," he said. "We still have to talk."

Kenny ushered her into the family room and she sat on the brown, corduroy couch. "Do you want something to drink?" he asked. When she shook her head, he sat next to her. "So what happened?"

"My divorce papers came in the mail yesterday," she said softly.

Kenny inclined his head slightly, then gathered Patsy in his arms. He had known Theo was somehow involved in her sadness. "I'm sorry you're hurting," he said, rubbing his hands across her shoulders. "Do you want to talk about it?"

Patsy held fast to Kenny. "There's nothing to talk about. My marriage was over long before I got this letter."

Kenny knew there was more, but he knew Patsy well enough to know she would only speak when she was ready. He held her and continued to stroke her arm.

"I loved him so much at one time," she began slowly. "How could this have happened to us, Kenny?"

He held her tighter, wishing he had some answers. "Who knows why things happen to people?"

Patsy knew he was thinking about Leah, and she immediately felt guilty. She only had to cope with a divorce; Kenny had to cope with being a widower. She pulled back from him and sat up. "I'm sorry for getting carried away."

He caressed her upper arms. "That's why friends have wide shoulders."

She smiled and he did, too.

He let his gaze travel from her new hairdo to her pumps. "I like your new look."

Patsy glanced down and brushed her hands across the soft leather of her skirt. "I needed to do something today to take the edge off the pain." She looked up at him, a self-deprecating smile tugging at her lips. "Enough about me. Do you know what Wendy asked me tonight?"

Kenny slumped back in the couch. "I can guess. She asked you if God was going to give her a new mommy."

"How'd you know?"

"She asked me the same question this morning over breakfast."

"Oh." Maybe Wendy's question was more serious than Patsy had thought.

"Yes, oh. That was all I could say, too."

She lifted her eyes to him. "Surely you said more to her than that, didn't you?"

Kenny sat up straighter and propped his elbows on his knees. Patsy was as protective of Wendy as a lioness of her cubs. "Like what? What do you think I should've said? She didn't seem overly concerned about it at the time."

Patsy's voice quickened. "You should have asked her what made her think of the question."

The corners of Kenny's mouth lifted. His Patsy was a lioness, all right. "Well, I did do that."

"And what did she say?"

Kenny took a deep breath. "She said Leah had told her God would send her a new mommy when the time was right."

"Do you really think Leah told her that?"

Kenny pinched the bridge of his nose. "I don't doubt it. Leah planned everything else. Why shouldn't she plan this, too?"

Patsy heard the annoyance in his voice. "You

shouldn't be angry with Leah. She only wanted the best for you and Wendy.''

Kenny folded his hands in front of him. "I know that, but talking to Wendy about a new mommy was a bit much, even for Leah.''

Patsy nodded, not in agreement but to acknowledge that she understood his feelings. "Leah loved you, Kenny. And you loved her. She'd want you to be happy.''

"You don't think I'm happy?''

Patsy shrugged her shoulders. She knew Kenny had to finish his grieving before he could be happy. She wasn't sure he'd done that yet. "Leah's been gone two years and to my knowledge you haven't even looked at another woman.''

"You're a fine one to talk," Kenny said. "How many dates have you had in the last two years?''

"I've been married for the last two years," Patsy said in defense of her actions.

"Right.''

Patsy sighed. She'd used her marriage as an excuse for not dating. And she hadn't been the one to file for a divorce because she didn't want her excuse taken away. "We're quite a pair, aren't we?''

He nodded, but didn't say anything.

"Wendy needs a mother, Kenny." Patsy said. "Even if you don't think you need a wife.''

"I know you're going to think this is selfish of me, Patsy, but I've always thought of you as Wendy's mother figure.''

Patsy thought that way, too, but she'd known, even before Wendy's question, that the child needed more. "Well, I'm glad, since I've felt like that myself. But Wendy needs more than an Aunt Patsy. She needs a mother. Someone who'll live here with the two of you. Someone who'll tuck her in every night. Someone who'll share her name and her father's love. That's not me, Kenny.''

Kenny studied her face for what seemed like minutes, before he countered, ''It could be.''

Chapter Three

Patsy didn't know what she'd expected Kenny to say, but that definitely wasn't it. "What did you say?"

Kenny stood and walked to the brick fireplace. He put his hands in his pockets and rocked back on his heels as the idea formed fully in his mind. "You heard me. You could be Wendy's new mommy."

"And your new wife?" Patsy asked, the amazement clear in her voice. She thought Kenny was losing his mind.

He took his hands out of his pockets and stretched them in the air. "Why not? You love Wendy. I love you. You love me."

"You love me?" she asked, incredulously.

He sat next to her again. "You know I do. You've been my best friend forever."

"We may love each other, Kenny, but we're not *in*

love. There's a big difference.'' Patsy stood and presented her back to him.

Kenny studied her, noticing again her long, shapely legs. ''Maybe... But you've told me over and over that passion doesn't make a marriage. You said friendship was more important. Well, we're friends.''

She turned around and glared at him, though she really wanted to scream. ''You can't really be serious about this.''

Kenny sat forward on the couch. ''Oh, but I am.'' Though the idea was new to him, he was sure about it. ''I know it sounds crazy, but think about it. You're already the closest thing to a mother that Wendy has. You spend more time with us than you do with anybody else, and God knows, you're the only woman *I* spend time with.''

He was serious. He was really serious. ''You'd do this for Wendy?''

''I'd do anything for Wendy.''

''Even marry a woman you don't love?''

He stood up and pulled her into his arms. ''But I do love you.''

''What makes you think I'd want to marry you?''

Kenny dropped his arms and stepped back. ''Why wouldn't you want to marry me? What's wrong with me?''

Patsy threw up her hands. ''That's not what I meant.'' She flopped back down on the couch, leaned her head back and closed her eyes. ''I can't believe we're having this conversation.''

''Yeah,'' Kenny said in a gruff voice. ''And I can't believe you're acting as though marrying me is the most awful thing that could happen to you.''

The hurt in his voice caused her to open one eye and

look at him. "I don't believe this. You're hurt because I won't consider this crazy idea?"

Kenny knew it was irrational, but he *was* hurt. "I'm not hurt."

"Sure you aren't. I know you, Kenny Sanders, and you're hurt. Why?"

"Because you act like the idea is so outrageous. It's not. I'm a good man and I'd make you a great husband. Why can't you even consider it?"

Patsy realized he was dead serious. "This isn't about whether you'd be a good husband, Kenny. It's about you suggesting that we turn a friendship into a marriage. That's what's so outrageous."

Kenny studied his folded hands. "It's a new thought, Patsy, but I don't think it's so outrageous. We'd be perfect for each other."

"And how do you figure that?" Patsy asked.

"First, Wendy gets her mother. Second, you get a marriage that's based on friendship and a man who really cares about you. Most marriages don't start out with odds that good."

"And what do you get, Kenny?"

"I get a mother for my daughter and a friend to share my life."

"You're serious about this?"

Kenny nodded. "I admit I haven't thought a lot about it, but it sounds right. Think about it."

"I *am* thinking about it and it sounds crazy."

"Why is it crazy?"

"Because we're friends, not lovers." She knew she was repeating herself, but she had to make him understand.

"Haven't you been telling me for the last two years

that friendship is the best basis for marriage? You've already had passion.''

That hurt, but before she could tell Kenny that, he spoke again. ''Besides it wouldn't have to be a real marriage. I need a mother for Wendy more than I need a wife.''

''Not a real marriage?'' she asked. This conversation was getting crazier and crazier by the moment.

''You know,'' he said, studying his hands again. ''No sex.''

Patsy laughed. At his words, at this entire conversation. ''No sex?''

He cleared his throat and looked up at her. ''Unless you want it, that is. I won't pressure you.''

Patsy shook her head slowly. She had to admit the thought of having sex with Kenny wasn't a new one. She'd thought about it more than once when they were growing up. In fact, she'd wanted Kenny to be the one to take her virginity. He'd been her best friend and she'd trusted him. Her adolescent mind had figured she and Kenny could do the deed and be done with it. She wouldn't have to think about it anymore. Of course, she'd never been able to mention this to Kenny. He was always too busy talking about other girls, and she did have some pride.

Kenny touched her knee. ''What are you thinking about?''

She moved her leg and his hand fell away. ''You and me. Married.''

''It wouldn't be so bad,'' Kenny said with a smug smile. ''Leah taught me to be a good husband.''

Leah's name brought new apprehensions. This *was* a ridiculous idea. ''You're still in love with her, aren't you?''

Kenny flecked a nonexistent speck from his pants. "She was my wife, the mother of my daughter. I'll always love her." That was true, but he knew what he left unsaid made him a liar.

Patsy heard what she thought was a tinge of grief in his voice, and it made her want to reach out and touch him. To comfort him. But she didn't dare. Not while they were having this conversation. "This marriage idea is not the right thing for us, Kenny. It's an easy answer, but I don't think it's the right one."

Kenny took her hands in his. "I know I sprang this on you out of the blue, but I'm very serious. I want for you to be my wife. To raise my daughter. You mean more to me than anyone else in the world, except Wendy. I think you know that."

Patsy looked at their intertwined fingers and a picture of their intertwined bodies flashed in her mind. She eased her hand out of his. "You're right. I care deeply for both you and Wendy. But marriage? That's a big step."

Kenny touched her cheek, a very familiar gesture, but somehow now it felt different. "Don't say no yet. Think about it some. We can talk tomorrow."

Patsy didn't believe thinking about it would help, but the pleading look in Kenny's eyes forced her to nod in agreement.

Kenny watched Patsy drive off in her brand-new BMW. She'd really gotten carried away today. No, he corrected himself, the purchase showed how much pain she'd been in. He was glad she'd splurged on herself. In his opinion, she didn't do enough of that. Once they were married, he'd make sure she did more of it.

He smiled. *Once they were married.* He knew Patsy

was resisting right now, but he also knew she'd come to her senses. That's the way she was. She had to think things through, go over all the angles. He half expected her to call him before she went to bed so they could talk about it. He knew the deciding factor for her would be the same as the deciding factor for him: Wendy.

Kenny tiptoed up the stairs and quietly entered his daughter's room. When he saw her curled up in bed, his heart expanded with the love he felt for her. He thanked God again that he'd come to his senses and realized how important time with her was. She'd enriched his life more than he ever could have imagined. Sadness enfolded him as thoughts of Leah flooded his mind.

Not a day went by that Kenny didn't regret the decision he'd made early in his marriage to devote so much of his time to work. How he wished he could get that time back. How he wished he could have shared it with Leah and Wendy. But he couldn't. And he had to live with that.

He also had to live with Leah's betrayal. That still haunted him. He was never going to be hurt like that again. That was the other reason marriage to Patsy was the right answer—she was his friend and she'd never hurt him. She loved him with a love that understood and didn't demand, and he loved her the same way. Patsy's was a safe kind of love. And that's exactly what he needed now.

Patsy gripped the steering wheel with both hands. She'd been driving around since leaving Kenny's house over an hour ago. How could he come up with such a ridiculous idea? The two of them married? What was he thinking?

She knew what he was thinking. He was figuring that

Wendy needed a mother and Patsy was a good choice. A safe choice. Yes, a safe choice because she wouldn't demand more from him than he was willing to give. He'd be able to hang on to his love for Leah as long as he wanted.

Patsy wasn't in love with Kenny and he wasn't in love with her, but they did love each other. Was that enough to make a marriage? She knew passion alone wasn't enough, but was friendship? As she remembered the pain of her failed marriage, she knew she could never again choose passion alone. And though she knew friendship alone wasn't the perfect choice, she felt safer with the idea of entering into a union based on what she shared with Kenny than doing so with the torrential emotions she'd shared with Theo. There was something comfortable, stable and, yes, safe about Kenny.

Patsy was surprised to look up and see she was near her street. She turned right onto Columbia Drive and headed to her house.

When she entered the kitchen, she automatically went to her answering machine on the counter. Four new messages. She knew without checking her Caller ID who had called. She looked anyway and found she was right: two calls from Kenny in the last hour.

Not wanting to hear what he had to say right now, she walked over and placed her handbag on the table. Before she was seated, the phone rang. Her heartbeat raced as she listened first to her taped greeting, then to the sound of Kenny's voice.

"Patsy, this is me again. Pick up the phone if you're there. Look, if you don't call me back tonight, I'm coming by your house after I take Wendy to school in the morning."

Kenny hung up, the answering machine clicked off

and Patsy expelled the sigh she hadn't realized she was holding. She couldn't speak with Kenny tonight. Tomorrow would be soon enough. Maybe. She still had a lot of thinking to do and she knew Kenny would only sway her. He was good at getting her to do what he wanted. He'd had enough practice during their childhood.

She got up from the table and made her way upstairs to the bedroom suite. She entered it, immediately kicked off her shoes and began undressing. She stopped when she saw her reflection in the full-length mirror her mom had given her for Christmas last year.

She made a critical appraisal of herself. The mirror showed the well-maintained body of a pretty, thirty-two-year-old woman. But tonight Patsy was looking at the person inside. She wanted the same things most women wanted—love, a successful career, a family. And she'd thought she would have it all with Theo. But that dream had shattered. And with it, she'd lost the part of herself that dared to dream.

Patsy stretched out on her bed and stared at the ceiling. She knew Kenny was still in love with Leah. Theirs was a love that even death and time couldn't conquer.

Leah... Patsy wondered what her friend would think of Kenny's marriage idea. At that moment the bedroom lights flickered off and on, and Patsy felt a cool breeze across her body.

"Take care of them for me, Patsy," a soft voice that sounded like Leah's said. "I'm counting on you."

"Leah?" Patsy called out. She sat up straight in the bed and looked around the room. Though the breeze had passed, she wrapped her arms around herself to ward off the chill she still felt. Was she hearing her own thoughts or was something else going on?

Patsy didn't know, but as she lay back down on the bed, a feeling of calm contentment enveloped her and her path became clear.

Kenny pulled into Patsy's driveway at eight-thirty the next morning. He spent a few moments gathering his thoughts, then got out of the car and made his way to her front door. He rang the bell once, and Patsy opened the door, almost as if she'd been waiting for him. Her welcoming smile made him smile.

"Come on in. I've got coffee on in the kitchen. Would you like a cup?" She didn't wait for his answer, but turned toward the kitchen.

He had no choice but to follow her. As he did, he couldn't help noticing the graceful sway of her hips under her terry-cloth bathrobe. He'd seen her in that robe many times before, but he didn't remember it outlining her figure the way it did this morning.

"So you've thought about my proposal?" he asked as soon as he was seated on one of the stools at her kitchen counter. He wanted her answer, but he also needed some conversation between them to keep his thoughts from dwelling on how long and sexy the back of her neck looked with her new, short hairdo.

She turned from the coffee maker to him. "What else could I think about?" she asked. "It's not every day that a woman gets a marriage proposal from her best friend and lifelong buddy."

Kenny blinked a few times. He wasn't sure what her sarcasm meant. "Have you decided?"

Her gaze bored into him and he felt as though she was looking into his soul. "I love Wendy like she's my own child."

"I know that," Kenny said, somewhat relaxed now

that she'd spoken. "And Wendy loves you just as much."

"I don't believe in divorce when children are involved, Kenny," she said. "And you don't have to ask why."

Kenny bowed his head slightly, remembering the quiet talks they'd shared as children when her parents were going through their divorce.

"If we do this," she continued, "it has to be forever. Or at least until Wendy's an adult. She can't lose another parent. It wouldn't be fair." Patsy took two mugs out of the cupboard and turned back to the coffee maker.

Kenny waited until she handed him a mug. "I agree with you. Wendy doesn't need to get another mother only to lose her." He put down his mug and reached for Patsy's hand. "That's why we're the perfect couple. We can last forever."

She removed her hand from his and lifted her mug to her lips. "What if you fall in love with somebody else?"

"It won't happen." Kenny wrapped his fingers around his coffee mug. "Being in love one time is more than enough."

Patsy wondered at his tone. It didn't sound like grief. "You're willing to bet your whole life on it?"

He placed the mug on the counter. "There's no risk. I know myself. But what about you? You could tie yourself up and miss out on the love of your life."

Theo's image appeared in her mind. She'd already had the love of her life. And lost it. "Like you said, being in love one time is more than enough."

Kenny merely nodded, running his fingers up and down the sides of his mug. He and Patsy were quite a pair. They'd make it work because they understood that friendship and commitment made a marriage. Being in love was an unnecessary extra. "You still haven't answered my question. Are you going to marry me?"

Patsy nodded. "I hope I don't live to regret this."

Kenny slid his stool back and stood up. "You won't, Patsy. I promise I'll do everything I can to make you happy."

She gave the barest hint of a smile. "And I'll do my best to be the finest mother Wendy could want."

Kenny noticed she didn't mention being a wife to him, and he was about to comment on it, but she spoke again.

"When do we tell Wendy?"

Chapter Four

"We'll tell her soon, but first we need to talk." Kenny took Patsy's hand and pulled her down on the stool next to his. "I'm happy you agreed to marry me, and I promise I'll be a good husband to you."

Patsy looked away and would have tugged her hand out of his but he tightened his hold.

"This isn't going to work if you're going to go shy on me. We've never held back with each other. That's what makes our friendship special. We can't let marriage ruin that."

Patsy looked up at him and wondered if they were doing the right thing. The caress of Kenny's thumb against the palm of her hand assured her they were. "It feels funny."

"Funny?"

She nodded. "Funny. Different. I can't explain it."

Kenny smiled, flashing the dimples she found irresistible on both him and Wendy, and her heart quickened. "I think I know what you mean," he said. "We've been friends for so long we've learned to ignore the fact that we're a man and a woman. And you're a very attractive woman, Patsy."

She took a deep breath. The compliment warmed her insides. "You're not so bad yourself."

Kenny squeezed her hand, then pulled her close to his chest as he'd often done in the past. "I believe in my heart that this is the right thing for us. I'll be the best husband I can be. You'll never regret marrying me. I promise you that."

"I know," Patsy mumbled into his shoulder. "This is what I want, too." She wanted to add that she also thought it was what Leah wanted, but she didn't. Maybe she would tell Kenny about her strange encounter later, if the moment seemed right.

Kenny pulled back from her. "So when do you want to get married?"

"I don't see any need to wait, do you?" Waiting time meant more thinking time, and she didn't want to think about her decision anymore.

Kenny grinned, and she knew she'd given the right answer. "How soon?" he asked.

"Week after next, maybe. My current project will be finished and I'll be able to take some time off to get moved into your place. What about you?"

"I should be able to clear my calendar. The Thompson case should wrap up by Friday." He paused, then asked, "What are you going to tell your mother?"

Patsy covered her mouth with her hand. Her mother would think she'd lost her mind. "I hadn't even thought about Mama."

"I'll go with you to tell her if you want me to," he offered.

Patsy removed the hand from her mouth. She'd agreed to this marriage, and fear of her mother wasn't going to make her change her mind. "That would be great, Kenny. Having both of us there should remove any reservations she may have about the suddenness of our plans." She paused. "I also have to call my father."

"Do you think he'll come?"

"Of course," she answered quickly. "He's a long-distance father, but he's still my dad. Are you going to tell Leah's parents?"

Kenny snapped his fingers. "I'd almost forgotten. They'll be here in a couple of weeks for Wendy's birthday. Where's your calendar?"

Patsy got up and handed Kenny the calendar from the cabinet next to the wall oven.

He took it and studied the dates. "Let's see. Wendy's grandparents get in on Saturday, the tenth, a week before Wendy's birthday, and they leave that same night to take Wendy on a week-long trip to Disney World. It's perfect, actually. We'll get married on the tenth. They'll leave for Orlando that night. We'll start our honeymoon the next day, Sunday, and we'll have Wendy's birthday party on the Saturday after they get back from Orlando."

"Honeymoon?"

Kenny tapped his forefinger to the tip of her nose. "Yes, honeymoon. That time the couple spends together after the wedding."

"Wedding?"

Kenny grinned, looking at her as if she'd gone crazy. "When people get married, they usually have a wedding."

Usually, Patsy thought. Her and Theo's wedding had

been a grand affair, the wedding young girls dream about. But what good had it done? It hadn't made their marriage last. "Why don't we have a small ceremony with just our closest friends and family? We've both had big weddings before. Let's make this one different in its simplicity."

"If that's what you want."

"It's what I want."

Kenny nodded his agreement. "Now, back to the honeymoon. Where do you want to go?"

Patsy nibbled her lower lip, and Kenny marveled that he'd never noticed how enticing she looked when she did so. "Why do we have to go anywhere?" she asked. "I have to move in with you. That week will give me a chance to get settled without disrupting Wendy's life too much."

"But don't you want to go somewhere?" Kenny asked again. Moving wasn't exactly his idea of a honeymoon. He'd promised himself he'd splurge on Patsy, and here she was talking about moving when he was talking about taking a trip.

"Why do we need to go someplace? What would we do on a honeymoon?"

Kenny's thoughts went immediately to what people usually did on a honeymoon, and he realized why a traditional one wasn't quite appropriate for him and Patsy. He shrugged. "I hadn't really thought about it, but people normally go on a honeymoon when they get married."

"But this isn't a normal marriage. We don't need a honeymoon, Kenny, we need a period of adjustment. Some time for us to get used to living in the same house."

"Won't people be suspicious if we don't go somewhere?'' Kenny asked, not quite liking the all-business approach Patsy was taking and not knowing why it bothered him.

"What people? My mother and your in-laws will think we're honeymooning at home, since Wendy will be away.''

"All right, all right. No honeymoon. I'll leave the wedding plans to you. Pick a time and place and I'll be there.''

She gave him a light punch in the shoulder. "You'd better be. I know where you live, remember?''

"You won't mind living in my house, will you? We could move in here if you'd like that better.''

"No, no,'' Patsy said, appreciating Kenny's thoughtfulness and knowing it boded well for their future. "Wendy needs the stability of her home. She's been through too much. Your house is home for her.''

"You're sure?''

"I'm sure,'' Patsy said, knowing she was right about Wendy's needs. Their house was practically a second home to her already. At the same time, Patsy was glad Kenny and Wendy no longer lived in the house they'd shared with Leah.

"Okay, that's settled. Are you going to ask Marilyn to stand up for you?''

"Who else? She's my second-best friend. And I guess you're asking Derrick?''

Kenny nodded. He and Derrick had become close friends when he'd worked in the district attorney's office. Now, Derrick was the district attorney, and Kenny ran a private practice from his home and a small office downtown. "He's the closest thing I have to a brother.''

Patsy's heart contracted with sympathy. Kenny had endured so much, had lost so much. First his parents had been killed in a car accident and he'd found out he was adopted. Then he'd lost Leah. Patsy's heart filled with determination to see that he didn't lose anything else. He deserved a happy, stable and safe home. And she could give him that; she was sure of it. "You, Wendy and I will be a family, Kenny. We'll always be there for each other."

He squeezed her hand. "You bet your bottom dollar we will."

Patsy looked at their joined hands and again a picture of their joined bodies formed in her mind. She gave a silent prayer of thanks that she wouldn't have to deal with that part of their marriage yet. She glanced up at Kenny's face. "Thank you," she said.

"For what?"

"For being considerate about our sharing the same bed, sleeping together. It certainly takes the pressure off."

He shrugged as if it wasn't that big a deal. "There's no need for us to rush. We can wait until you're ready."

Patsy couldn't help it, she laughed.

"What's so funny?"

"You. We'll wait until *I'm* ready, you said. How do you know you'll be ready when I'm ready?"

Kenny grinned at her. "It'll be a hardship, but I think I'll be able to force myself to get up for it."

Her eyes widened and her mouth dropped open. "You'll force yourself..." She raised her fist to punch him again. Harder.

He caught her hand in his and started to laugh. "Where's your sense of humor? I was joking."

She jerked her hand out of his. He'd voiced one of her unspoken fears—what if Kenny wasn't sexually attracted to her? "Well, you have a warped sense of humor! That wasn't even close to being funny."

"You're getting married?" Derrick's eyes widened and he lowered the soda can from his lips. "When did you start seeing somebody? Who is she?"

Kenny stepped back from Derrick's desk and raised his arms in mock protest. "Hold on, Mr. District Attorney, this is not a courtroom."

"Sorry, man." Derrick placed his can on the desk, pushed back his chair and folded his arms across his flat stomach, the picture of calm. "But you can't spring news like this on a guy. You should've given me some warning."

Kenny grinned, then propped his hip against the edge of Derrick's desk. He didn't buy Derrick's calm pose for a minute. He knew it took all his friend's patience, and then some, to stop the barrage of questions. "How could I give you warning when I didn't have any?"

Kenny noticed Derrick's hands tightening. "You didn't have..." his friend began, his voice rising with each word. Kenny lifted a brow and Derrick lowered his voice. "You've got to explain. First tell me *who* you're going to marry."

"Patsy," Kenny said, then held his breath. Derrick was his closest friend, after Patsy. And he wanted his support, if not his approval.

"Patsy?" Derrick jumped up from his chair and grabbed Kenny's arm in a powerful handshake. "It's about time you did something right."

"What's that supposed to mean?"

Derrick dropped back down in his chair, a big grin covering a face most women found so handsome they fell all over themselves the first time they saw him. "It means, my friend, that I never thought you and Patsy would be smart enough to figure out that you were in love with each other."

"In love? Me and Patsy?"

"Don't sound surprised. Evidently you came to the same conclusion or you wouldn't be getting married."

Kenny didn't respond.

Derrick leaned forward in his chair. "Let me repeat that. Evidently you came to the same conclusion or you wouldn't be getting married...?"

Kenny still didn't say anything.

"Okay," Derrick said. "This is where you're supposed to say, 'Yeah, man,' or something similar."

Kenny stood up and shoved his hands in his pockets. "I do love Patsy. I've always known that."

Derrick dropped his head on the desk. "Oh, man, why do I know there's a 'but' in there somewhere?"

His friend's exaggerated antics made Kenny smile. "Patsy and I love each other, but we're not *in love* with each other."

Derrick lifted his head from the desk and stared at his friend, amazement in his eyes. "You love each other, but you're not in love with each other. What the hell is that supposed to mean? Either you love her or you don't."

Kenny expelled a deep sigh. If he didn't know how Derrick's analytical mind worked, he'd guess his friend was deliberately being obtuse. "What I'm trying to tell you is that Patsy and I are getting married because Wendy needs a mother, not because we're in love."

"And Patsy went for that?" Before Kenny could respond, Derrick added, "Don't bother to answer. I already know what you'll say. Patsy loves you so much that I have no doubt she agreed to this ridiculous arrangement." He lifted a brow at Kenny. "She *is* going to move in with you, isn't she?"

"Of course. We're getting married. Where else would she live?"

Derrick's grin reappeared. "And you'll be sharing the same bed?"

Kenny didn't answer.

"Don't tell me you aren't going to sleep in the same bed." When Kenny still didn't respond, Derrick shook his head in disgust. "If Patsy were living under my roof, you can bet I'd be doing everything in my power to get her in my bed. But you're going to make her your wife and then not sleep with her? You've lost your mind."

"I haven't," Kenny said too quickly, and immediately recognized how childish he sounded. But what Derrick was saying made his arrangement with Patsy sound ridiculous. And he didn't like it. "Eventually we'll sleep together, but Patsy will choose the time."

"She said she didn't want to sleep with you after you got married?"

Kenny shrugged his shoulders. Derrick's grilling was beginning to wear on him. "Not exactly. I kinda told her that I wouldn't pressure her to sleep with me until she was ready."

"You're not attracted to her?"

"Don't be stupid. Of course I'm attracted to her." Patsy was the first woman he'd thought about making love to since Leah's death. The only reason he'd joked when she'd asked about his being ready to make love when she was ready was that he didn't want to scare her or rush her. "Patsy's a beautiful woman. Inside and out."

"Then why did you make that suggestion about the separate beds?"

"Because I didn't want her to feel pressured. A part of me feels like a selfish bastard for taking advantage of her. I know she only agreed to this marriage because she loves Wendy. But I'll make sure she never regrets it. I'll make her happy or die trying."

"You're a fool, Kenneth Sanders," Derrick said, shaking his head. "Separate beds? And you've been married before. I don't understand it."

Kenny got up from the desk, tired of Derrick and his negative comments. "You don't have to understand it. Patsy and I understand it. We're getting married and I want you to be my best man, if it doesn't go against your principles."

"I think you're a fool, but I wouldn't miss this wedding for the world. You and Patsy may think you're entering into a union of the mind, but mark my words, that misconception will be corrected in short order. Now when's the big day?"

"Have you told your mother?" Marilyn asked from her seat on the wooden bench behind the playground swings. She and Patsy were eating lunch while her preschool class played.

"I thought I'd tell you first."

Marilyn took a bite of the six-inch tuna sub Patsy had bought for her. "Uh-huh."

"Uh-huh, nothing. I'm meeting Kenny at her house when I leave here."

Marilyn wiped the crumbs from her lips, then brushed off the ones that had landed on the skirt of her classic shirtdress. "Bringing reinforcements along, huh? You're afraid to tell Mae, aren't you?"

"Not afraid, exactly. Maybe more like leery. Mama practically forced Theo and me to have a long engagement. If I hadn't thought it would break her heart, we would've eloped." Patsy shrugged, remembering the heated argument they'd had when her mother learned she and Theo were getting married. "She thought we decided too quickly."

"And you think she'll feel the same way about you and Kenny?"

"Maybe. I just don't want to get into it with her. I'm feeling good about what Kenny and I are about to do and I don't want Mama to bring me down. Maybe with both of us present she won't ask so many questions."

"She won't. I think she has a crush on Kenny herself. Your mom always did have a soft spot for that smooth talker."

Patsy smiled at her friend's words. "Mama and Kenny have a good relationship, but I don't know what she's going to think of this quick marriage."

"Well, I for one think it's great. I've always thought you and Kenny belonged together."

"Yeah, right," she said, not putting too much stock in Marilyn's words. Patsy had debated telling Marilyn the real reason for her and Kenny's quick decision, but in the end she'd done so. "Kenny and Leah belonged together. Kenny and I will be together because we love Wendy."

"Keep telling yourself that. Kenny has deeper feelings for you than either of you realize."

"Kenny's still in love with Leah," Patsy retorted. "I don't think he's let go of his grief yet. He cares about me, but he's *in love* with Leah. I've always accepted that."

"You're not being honest with yourself. Don't you remember how jealous you were of Leah when she first moved here?"

Patsy remembered, all right. "I was a little jealous," she admitted.

"A little?" Marilyn rolled her eyes toward the sky. "You're rewriting history, girl. Try more like a lot."

Patsy knew her friend was right. She'd almost made a fool of herself when the beautiful Leah had moved to Grove City. A tenth grader like herself, Kenny and Marilyn, Leah had immediately captured Kenny's eye and his heart. They had quickly become a couple, and much to the young Patsy's dismay, she'd finally had a rival for Kenny's affection. Not that she'd thought about Kenny that way. Well, at least she hadn't thought about him that way *much*. Kenny was her friend, her best friend, and until Leah no one had come between them.

Leah's arrival in Grove City had marked a turning point in Patsy's relationship with Kenny. Before Leah, she'd thought of Kenny as hers in a proprietary way that only a youngster could. But with Leah around things changed. Not only did Kenny want to spend all his time with her, Leah was all he wanted to talk about when he and Patsy did get together. "You're a girl, Patsy. What do you think she'd like?" or "You're a girl, Patsy. Why is she acting like this?" became his theme song.

Many times Patsy had wanted Kenny to tell Leah to kiss off. And a couple of times he'd done it. But he'd been so miserable afterward that Patsy had wished they'd get back together. It was after their second breakup that she and Leah had become friends. When Patsy saw that the girl was as miserable without Kenny as he was without her, her heart had softened and she was able to find a place in it for Leah.

"But all that jealousy was before we all became friends," Patsy finally said to Marilyn. "Leah turned out to be a very nice girl."

Marilyn brushed the crumbs off her hands and put the remains of her sandwich in the brown bag on the bench next to her. "She was all right."

"All right? Now that's an understatement. She made the varsity cheering squad the first year she tried out. She was homecoming queen junior *and* senior year and class beauty *every* year."

"I know," Marilyn said, standing up. "I was the one she beat out for homecoming queen senior year."

"You're not still upset about that, are you?"

"Not really." Marilyn signaled her aide to round up the students. "A person couldn't stay mad with Leah. She was too nice. Sometimes I wished she wasn't so nice, then I'd have had a reason not to like her."

Patsy chuckled. "I know what you mean. I wanted to dislike her, too. But I couldn't. Leah was about as close to perfect as a person could get." As Patsy said the words, she realized what big footsteps she'd be stepping into as Kenny's wife. He wasn't in love with her, and she accepted that, but what if he began comparing her to Leah and she always came up short?

Marilyn snapped her fingers in Patsy's face. "Where are you?"

Patsy shook her head to clear the thoughts that tried to take away her joy, then stood. "I'm here."

Marilyn peered into her eyes, and Patsy let her gaze slide away. "You're here, but your thoughts were miles away."

"Sorry. I was thinking about Mama."

"More like dreading your conversation with her," Marilyn said. "But I have a gut feeling she's going to surprise you this time. I bet I'm not the only one who thought you and Kenny would have gotten together if Leah hadn't come to town."

Patsy picked up their discarded paper bags from the bench and tossed them into the garbage can closest to them. "I don't like the sound of that. You make it seem as though I'm a vulture coming in for the kill now that Leah is out of the picture. It's not like that. I grew to love Leah almost as much as I love Kenny. I wish she were still here for him and Wendy. They need her so much. But she's not. And I'm going to do what I can to make their lives better. I don't want them to forget her. I only want them to be happy. They deserve it, after all they've gone through." And I know Leah understands this, she added to herself.

"Everything you say is right. I know that. But it doesn't make what I say any less true. You and Kenny were destined to be together. Don't look at yourself as a substitute for Leah. Kenny loves you more than he realizes."

"Don't—" Patsy began.

"It's true, though," Marilyn interrupted as she watched her preschoolers line up for the trip back to the classroom. "And I think that, somewhere deep inside, you know it. I'll always believe that you married Theo because Kenny married Leah."

The words hit Patsy like a punch in the stomach. "Some friend you are. How can you think I'd be so shallow as to do that?"

Marilyn motioned to her classroom aide to direct the kids back to class. "Don't get mad at me. I don't think you're shallow. You're human. And like most humans you do what you can to deal with the pain in your life. Theo was your pain reliever." Marilyn paused. "I have to get back to work. Go talk to your mother. I bet she'll be happy for you and Kenny."

Patsy stared after her friend as she joined the aide in

leading the kids back inside. *Theo was your pain reliever*, Marilyn had said. The words rolled around in Patsy's mind, and she knew they weren't true. She'd married Theo because she loved him, not because Kenny had married Leah.

She glanced down at her watch. She'd have to rush to get to her mother's house before Kenny did. She grabbed her purse from the bench and strode off to her car, the words, *Theo was your pain reliever*, still floating around in her mind.

Chapter Five

The battered blue pickup Kenny had kept running since high school was in the driveway when Patsy drove up to her mother's house. She sucked in a deep breath, dreading the conversation to come.

She walked around to the kitchen entrance and stopped when she saw a smiling Kenny seated at the kitchen table with her mother, a plate of chocolate fudge in front of him. Kenny said something and her mother blushed. Had he already told her? Patsy wondered.

When she opened the door, both of them stopped talking and looked at her. Kenny's broad chest and long legs, covered by a tan sweater and matching slacks, affected her as much now as they had when he'd come to her house first thing this morning. She hoped she'd be able to hide her response to him now, as she'd done then.

"Did I interrupt something?" she asked, taking a seat at the table.

Kenny grinned at her, then grabbed her hands and pulled her to him. The kiss started slowly, but he quickly deepened it. When she would have tugged her hands away so she could touch him, he ended the kiss, but kept her hands firmly in his.

"I've been telling your mother about our plans, sweetheart." He squeezed her fingers and she felt the tingle all the way up her arm.

Our plans? she asked him with her eyes. Before she could form a response, her mother leaned over and hugged her. "I'm so happy for you, darling. I've always wanted you and Kenny to find each other." She beamed at Kenny. "And now he tells me you're getting married. It's wonderful."

Patsy shot Kenny a glance that plainly asked, *What have you told her?*

He squeezed her hand again.

"But I'm disappointed in you, Patsy," her mother continued, and Patsy felt her heart tighten. She opened her mouth to explain that they were getting married for Wendy's sake, but before she could speak, Mae said, "How awful of you to keep secrets from your mother. You should have told me you and Kenny were falling in love."

Patsy turned widened eyes on Kenny.

He kissed her again, this time allowing his lips to linger against hers. "Now, don't be mad," he said. "I couldn't wait until you got here. I had to tell her."

She wanted to place her fingers to her lips to stop their throbbing, but Kenny still held her hands. Instead, she stared at him and wondered why he kept kissing her. Okay, maybe she also thought about how good his kissing was.

"You two make me so happy," her mother said, dabbing at her eyes with a napkin from the plastic holder in the middle of the table. "This is what I've always wanted for you, Patsy—a man who understands the meaning of loving a woman. Kenny told me he never thought he could love another woman after Leah, but he loves you."

Patsy shook her hand loose from Kenny's and embraced her weeping mother. "Oh, Mama," she pleaded, "don't cry."

Her mother choked back her tears, then pulled away to look at her. "I worried so much about you, Patsy. I wondered if my divorce had scarred you for life. And then when you and Theo decided to get a divorce, I thought I was right. But yesterday, I began to get hopeful. When you bought your new car and cut your hair, I thought it was a sign you were coming back to life. And now I know why." She cast a meaningful glance at Kenny. "Now that you and Kenny have found each other, I know you'll have the kind of life and love that I've always wanted for you."

Patsy didn't know what to say. She shot a quick glance at Kenny, but his eyes showed how much he was lost for words, too. She knew he felt as guilty as she did for the fraud they were perpetrating on her mother, but they had gone too far to change their story now.

"And Wendy will be my first grandchild," her mother continued. "But hopefully not my last. I want to fill this house with the sounds of my grandchildren's laughter." She winked at Kenny. "Think you can handle that?"

Children, Patsy thought. She and Kenny hadn't talked about children. She was sure she wanted more, but she didn't know what Kenny's thoughts were. What if Wendy was enough for him? She held her breath while she waited for his answer.

Kenny looked up at her mother and flashed his brightest smile. "No doubt about it, Mrs. Mae. No doubt about it."

A cacophony of emotions spread through Patsy as she and Kenny discussed with her mother the small ceremony they wanted. By the time they were almost done, Patsy was pretty close to believing that what she and Kenny had was a love match.

She peeked up at him while her mother pared down the guest list to fifteen—the number of guests Kenny's house could comfortably accommodate for the wedding and the reception dinner they planned. His response was a smile and a quick squeeze of her hand. She wondered if he noticed the shiver his touch caused.

"You're not cold, are you?" her mother asked with concern. "Early spring is the worst time of the year to get a cold."

Patsy pulled her gaze away from Kenny and turned to reassure her mother. "I'm fine, Mama. Now, what else do we have to decide?"

Thankfully, her mother dropped her question and focused again on the wedding plans. Patsy tried to listen, and somehow she was able to keep up with the conversation, but her mind was still on Kenny. As friends, they'd always been touchers, but not like this. Her lips still burned from his kisses, and her hand felt so hot she wanted to dunk it in a bucket of cold water. What was wrong with her? she wondered.

Kenny was glad he didn't have to pretend to listen to the wedding plans. He couldn't have if his life depended on it. Not with Patsy sitting next to him, nervously nibbling her recently kissed lips. When he'd kissed her the first time, it had been for her mother's benefit. He'd planned a casual touching of their lips to reassure Mrs. Mae that what he and Patsy shared was real. But the kiss hadn't happened as he'd planned. As soon as his lips had touched her soft, full ones, he'd been lost. God, her lips were so lush and so sweet. He could have caressed them all afternoon.

He shook his head slightly. No, he couldn't have. He would have wanted more after a while. Hell, who was he kidding? He'd wanted more while he was kissing her. He'd increased the pressure of the kiss for that very reason. He hadn't meant to do it, but his tongue had pushed against her lips almost as if it had a mind of its own. Something inside him had broken when her soft lips parted so invitingly for him. And then he was inside, exploring the contours of Patsy's sweet, sweet mouth.

Kenny shifted in his chair at the unbidden and, at this time, unwelcome thoughts of the natural result of a kiss like that shared between a man and the woman he was about to marry. How would it feel to make love with Patsy? he wondered.

He closed his eyes and saw a picture of Patsy naked, her short hair perfectly framing a face so dear it took his breath away. He forced his brain to stay focused on her face, not wanting to battle his body's natural response if his mind's eye traveled the length of her naked form.

Focus on her face, he repeated in his mind. Her dark skin, so smooth, so clear, so soft. Yes, so very soft. He still remembered the feel of her lips against his. How could he have held Patsy in his arms all those many times and never noticed her softness? he wondered.

And her eyes. Patsy's eyes were truly the window to her soul. She couldn't hide anything, at least not from him. It had been true when they were children and it was still true now. He remembered the questions that had plagued her after he kissed her. She'd looked so bewildered that he'd wanted to laugh. Actually, he'd wanted to kiss her again. He'd taken his first opportunity and done so. And he wanted to do so again. And again.

Kenny knew what that meant. He wanted Patsy. He wanted to make love to his best friend. Okay, he admitted, this wasn't the first time the idea had crossed his mind. But in the past, he'd felt dirty for thinking about Patsy that way. She'd been his best friend, almost like a sister, so he'd quickly brushed his sensual thoughts aside. And he had kept them away for years. He hadn't thought of Patsy in that way since before he'd married Leah. And he hadn't wanted another woman, not a woman with a face, in the two years since Leah had died.

Until now. Now his body was alive with desire for Patsy. The feeling invigorated him. He had wondered if he'd ever feel intense sexual attraction again. Well, now he knew.

His eyes opened slowly and his lips turned downward. Maybe Derrick was right. Maybe he had been a fool to give Patsy the option of not sharing his bed until she was ready. They planned to spend the rest of their lives together, so what was the point in waiting?

He felt her gaze on him and glanced over at her.

"So what do you think?" she asked, the question clear in her eyes.

He couldn't answer, because he had no idea what she was talking about.

"Just like a man," her mother chided. "You haven't heard a word we've said, have you, Kenny?"

Kenny reached for Patsy's hand again, this time pulling it to his lips for a soft kiss. "I told Patsy this part was hers. I trust her with my life and my child. Surely I can trust her to plan our wedding.''

Patsy walked back to her car on legs so limp she prayed with each step they wouldn't fail her before she reached the vehicle. If only Kenny would take his hand off her waist. His touch was distracting to the point of being dangerous. What in the world was wrong with her? What was wrong with him?

She stole a quick glance at him as he talked with her mother, who was following them to their cars. Patsy knew his touch was for her mother's benefit, but that didn't make it any less potent. Her red silk blouse provided no defense against the heat of his touch.

''We'll bring Wendy by sometime this week, Mrs. Mae,'' Kenny was saying. ''I know she'll love spending some time with her new grandmother.''

Patsy didn't have to look to know a wide smile was spreading across her mother's face. The older woman couldn't love Wendy any more than she already did.

''You be sure to do that,'' she responded. ''And drive safely.''

Kenny made the appropriate responses before opening Patsy's door and helping her into the car. A soft sigh escaped her lips when he closed it. Now she could pull herself together again.

Kenny's knock on her window brought her attention back to him. She started the engine and pressed the button to roll the window down.

''Once more for your mother,'' Kenny said, leaning in her window and giving her another kiss. This one was so sweet and light that she wondered if he'd kissed her or if she'd dreamed it.

Kenny's ''You follow me'' brought her attention back

to the present. She waved at her mom, rolled up the car window and, when Kenny backed out of the driveway, did as he'd asked.

The drive from her mother's house to his took twenty minutes, but it wasn't long enough for Patsy to get her bearings. Before she could get out of the car, Kenny had opened her door and extended his hand to help her.

She ignored his offer and got out under her own strength. "There's no one watching. You can stop the playacting," she said.

Kenny dropped his hand. "I'm sorry about your mother, but I couldn't tell her the real reason for our wedding. You saw her. It's been years since I've seen her that happy."

Patsy brushed her hands down her navy linen skirt before looking up at him. Her mother had certainly been happy. She and Kenny had been joking like they had done before all the sadness. Though the older woman was attractive with her graying hair and slightly plump figure, a tinge of sadness usually shaded her eyes. That sadness hadn't been present today. "You could have waited until I got there."

"Come on, Pats," he said, tugging on her arm, a contrite smile on his face. "You know I'm a pushover where your mother is concerned. Once she gave me that chocolate, I was a goner."

She felt her anger begin to recede and cursed herself. Kenny was up to his old tricks. She punched a slim, coral-painted nail into his chest. "Not this time, buster." She dropped her hand and strode toward the front door.

"What do you mean, not this time?" he asked, rushing after her.

When she reached the locked front door, she turned

and faced him. "You know exactly what I mean. Your puppy-dog demeanor is not going to make me cave in."

Kenny reached around her and unlocked the door, then pushed it open and let her in before him. When she turned around in the foyer, he had the nerve to sport a grin. "And what are you grinning about?" she asked.

He folded his arms across his wide chest and leaned back against the closed front door, his intoxicating grin still in place. "Nothing."

"Yeah, right. Come off of it, Kenny. I know you."

He unfolded himself from the door, dropped an arm around her shoulders, ignoring her feeble protest, and led her into the family room. "You're upset about the kisses, aren't you?" he asked, when they were both seated on the couch.

She dropped her glance from his. "Not exactly."

He laughed, but when she glared at him, he stopped. "Sorry about that. The laughing, not the kissing. I had to kiss you to make your mother believe we were in love. Even though she was happy about our news, I could see she was skeptical. I had to prove to her that we were serious."

That sounded plausible to Patsy, but she didn't want to let Kenny off too easily. "Well, you could have told me."

"When? You were late getting there. I had to play it by ear."

"Darn," she muttered to herself. She really hated allowing Kenny to have the last word. "There was no way you could have told her the real reason we're getting married?"

He relaxed back into the brown couch. "What was the point? We're getting married and we're staying married. I don't think the details are anybody's business but ours.''

Her talk with Marilyn came to mind. "What did you tell Derrick?''

"I told him we were getting married.''

"And what else?''

Kenny stood up and pushed his hands in his pockets, causing his pants to tighten around his firm buns. Patsy had to force her gaze higher on his anatomy.

"Did you tell him the details?'' she asked, when he didn't answer.

"Yeah.''

"And what did he say?''

Kenny shrugged. "He said congratulations and then he agreed to be my best man.''

"Now I know you're lying. Derrick doesn't know how to *not* ask questions.''

Kenny turned to her and lifted his arms in supplication. "What could he say? He wants me to be happy. You make me happy. End of story. What did Marilyn say?''

Patsy wasn't about to tell Kenny that. As usual, her friend had said too much. "She was surprised, but she agreed to be my maid of honor. She's happy for us.''

"That's all? Megamouth Marilyn had no words of advice, no sage wisdom to pass your way?''

Patsy smiled at his description of Marilyn. Most men would have talked about her friend's clear, brown complexion or her warm, doelike eyes or her movie-star figure. But not Kenny. "Marilyn's Marilyn. She's okay with it and she's happy for us.''

Kenny took his hands out of his pockets and came to sit next to Patsy on the couch again. "You can still back out,'' he said softly, looking at his folded hands.

The tenor of his voice touched a chord deep within her. "Do you want to back out?"

He looked at her. "No way. The more I think about this, the more I know it's right." He reached for her hand, and when she placed it in his, covered it with his other one. "I know we can be happy together. But we have to be honest with each other, keep the lines of communication open. If I do something that bothers you, tell me. And if I don't hear you, tell me again."

Patsy wondered if her shyness earlier had prompted him to make this request.

"Promise you'll do that?" he asked when she didn't say anything.

"When have you known me not to tell you when you were out of line, Kenny Sanders?" she said, intentionally using a tone designed to make him lighten up a little.

He squeezed her fingers and gave her the smile she wanted. "You have a point there."

Kenny didn't say anything more and Patsy didn't have anything to add, so they remained silent. A few minutes later, Kenny broke the silence.

"I meant what I told your mother." At the question in her eyes, he continued, "About children. I'd like for us to have more. When you're ready. You do still want children, don't you?"

Hope long dormant sprang up in her. Yes, she still wanted children. Happy children, like Wendy. "I think so, Kenny," she hedged, "but let's take this a little slower. Yesterday we were best buddies and today we're talking marriage and babies. We're moving too fast."

"I'm not rushing you. I just wanted you to know that I'd like this to be a real marriage in every sense of the word."

Something in his voice made her tense up. "So do I, but I think you had the right idea when you suggested we take it slowly. I'm not ready yet for more than moving in here and becoming a mother to Wendy. It's going to be awhile before I'm ready to be a wife."

"You're afraid, aren't you?"

He knew her too well. "Maybe marrying your best friend isn't such a good idea," she said, only half-jokingly. "I don't think I'll be able to have any secrets around you."

"And neither will you be able to dodge my questions. Now, what are you afraid of?"

She sighed, then decided it was either tell him now or have him badger her to death. "I don't want to lose our friendship. Right now, it's the most precious relationship in my life. I don't know what I'd do if I lost it."

"You're not going to lose my friendship."

"I will if you want me to step into Leah's shoes. I'm not her."

"I never said you were her," Kenny said, clearly offended. "I'd never pretend you were Leah or want you to step into her shoes. You have your own place in my heart. A place that was yours even when Leah was alive."

Patsy knew she had to tread softly here, but she couldn't back down. "You haven't even looked at another woman since Leah died, and now we're getting married and talking about babies. It's too quick, Kenny. We need to let our relationship evolve slowly to the loving marriage we both want."

"You do think that'll happen, don't you?"

She smiled. "Of course I do. I wouldn't have agreed to marry you if I didn't. But it's very important to me that we build a strong foundation that's not complicated by..."

"Sex?" he offered, when she didn't finish.

She nodded, though she was really thinking passion. Passion like she'd shared with Theo.

"You understand, though, that ours won't be a real marriage until we make that step of sexual intimacy?"

"I understand. And it'll happen, but in its own time." She shrugged. "We could always postpone the marriage until that time comes, if you want."

"No," Kenny said quickly. "Let's get married now. Waiting won't change anything."

Patsy released a breath. For reasons she didn't want to investigate, it was important to her that Kenny hadn't wanted to wait. Very important.

Chapter Six

"Carrie Williams calls her new mommy Mama Doris," Wendy said from her seat across the table from Patsy and Kenny. Chocolate ice cream covered her lips. "Can I call you Mama Patsy?"

Immediately, tears of joy welled up in Patsy's eyes, and she felt Kenny's hand caress her shoulder. The tears had been there since she and Kenny had first told Wendy of their marriage plans. The little girl had launched herself into Patsy's arms and hugged her tightly, telling her how glad she was that her aunt Patsy would become her new mommy. "Of course, sweetheart, I'd love it if you called me Mama Patsy."

Wendy bobbed her small head up and down. "Okay," she said, then dipped her spoon into her bowl of chocolate ice cream. It had been Wendy's idea to celebrate the news with dessert at her favorite ice-cream shop.

Patsy and Kenny couldn't deny her the treat. "Do I have to wait until after the wedding to call you Mama Patsy?"

Patsy looked at Kenny and he smiled.

"You can call me Mama Patsy anytime you want, sweetheart. You don't have to wait until after the wedding."

"Okay," Wendy said, smacking her lips together. "May I have more ice cream?"

Kenny laughed, but shook his head. "One bowl is enough for tonight, young lady. It's time we headed home."

"But Daddy," Wendy began, but his look stopped her. She focused on Patsy. "Mama Patsy, may I have more ice cream?"

Kenny covered his laugh with a cough while Patsy responded to Wendy. "I agree with your father. It's time for us to go home now."

Wendy pouted, then mumbled, "Carrie Williams's new mommy lets her have all the ice cream she wants."

Kenny looked over at Patsy. "Are you sure you want to do this?" he asked, his eyes twinkling with mirth.

Patsy punched him in the shoulder. "You can't back out now, buddy." She pushed her bowl away and leaned toward the six-year-old. "Wendy, your father and I are going to be a team, like your kick-ball team. We're going to love you and we're going to do what's best for you."

Wendy's eyes widened. "Does that mean I can have more ice cream?"

Kenny leaned forward as if to speak, but Patsy placed her hand on his wrist to stay him. "Let's think about kick ball. Do you remember the last game you played?"

Wendy bowed her head slowly. "We lost."

"And why did you lose?"

"Because Mary Willis tried to beat Carrie to the base instead of rolling the ball to me like Mrs. Rivers said. We would have won if Mary hadn't done that. She thinks she knows more than anybody. She should have done what Mrs. Rivers told her to do."

Patsy felt Kenny relax next to her.

"Well, your daddy and I are like a team. When he tells you something, I'm not going to tell you something different."

Wendy looked down at her empty ice-cream bowl, then lifted her alert eyes to Patsy. "I'm not going to get any more ice cream, am I?"

Patsy shook her head. "Do you know why?"

Wendy glanced at her father. "Because Daddy is the coach and we have to do what he tells us."

Patsy stomped on Kenny's foot when he laughed. Wendy hadn't quite captured what she meant and Patsy didn't know how to explain it to her. She looked at Kenny. "Your turn."

Kenny leaned forward and clasped his hands together on the table. "Mama Patsy and I are both coaches. We work together."

"And I'm the team?" Wendy said, her nose turned up as if she still didn't understand.

Kenny smiled at his daughter. "That's close enough."

"Now that that's settled," Patsy said to Wendy, "why don't the two of us go the bathroom and clean our faces?"

"Okay," she said, hopping down off her bench seat.

When Patsy got up to join her, Kenny tugged on her hand. "Good try," he said, his eyes dancing.

"Right. Next time I'll have to think of a better analogy."

"Let's go, Mama Patsy," Wendy urged. "My hands are sticky."

Kenny watched as Patsy led Wendy in the direction of the bathroom. The three of them were going to make it, he was sure. And that unpredictable bundle of joy that was his daughter was going to be the glue that kept them together.

Until they had more bundles of joy. A vision of a pregnant Patsy appeared in his mind, her full breasts fuller, her cheeks bright as blackberries, her stomach protruding with his child. In his mind, he reached out and lifted her maternity blouse, so he could touch her swollen belly. The touch—

"We're ready, Daddy," Wendy said, lifting her hands for him to see. "All clean."

Kenny dragged his attention to his daughter. "Good girl," he said, then tugged on one of her braids. "You ready?" he asked Patsy.

When she nodded, he stood up, pulled a few bills from his wallet and tossed them on the table. Wendy skipped to the door ahead of them and he placed his hand on Patsy's lower back to guide her out of the shop, giving her back the caress he'd wanted to give her stomach in his vision.

When they reached his car, Kenny opened the front door so Patsy could slide into the passenger seat. He didn't miss the expanse of smooth thigh exposed as she did so. He sure did like the new clothes she'd bought. The short skirts and her long legs really did a number on him. Shaking his head, he closed Patsy's door and opened the back door for Wendy. "Here you are, Peanut."

Wendy hopped up on the back seat.

"Buckle your seat belt," he reminded her.

She reached for the buckle and strapped herself in. Then she grinned up at her father. "Got it."

He rubbed his hand across her jaw. "Good girl." God, how he loved this child that looked so much like Leah. He closed Wendy's door, thinking of Leah and the years they'd shared. It had been a good life, he mused as he slid behind the steering wheel. They had been happy. At least, he'd been happy. Though he loved Leah, the ache of her betrayal still stuck with him. How could she have considered divorcing him?

"God bless Daddy and Mama Patsy and Grandma Ellis and Grandpa Ellis and Grandma Mae and Mrs. Walden," Wendy said, beginning her prayers. Kenny noticed that her list of people for God to bless seemed to be getting longer each night. Her latest addition was Grandma Mae, Patsy's mother.

"And God please say hi to Mommy and tell her that I love her and miss her. And tell her that I am so happy that Mama Patsy is my new mommy."

Kenny looked over at Patsy and thought he saw tears in her eyes. If either of them had questions about the rightness of their upcoming nuptials, Wendy had answered them with her prayers tonight. The little girl couldn't be happier with their news.

"And say hi to Grandma Sanders and Grandpa Sanders, too. Oh, and God, please tell Mommy that I got a new grandmother, too. She didn't tell me about that. Amen."

Wendy hopped up from her knees and jumped into bed. "I can't wait till tomorrow so I can tell Carrie Williams about my new mommy and my new grandmother. Can Mrs. Walden, Carrie Williams and Audrey Simmons, and Meg Thomas and Hillary Benson come to the wedding party, too?''

Patsy smiled down at her. "Some of your friends can come, but not all of them. You can invite them to your birthday party the following week." She leaned over and kissed Wendy on the cheek. "Now get some sleep, sweetheart. You've had a busy day. We'll talk more about the wedding tomorrow."

"I'm not tired, Mama Patsy. Let's talk about the wedding and the party now."

"Wendy..." Kenny began.

"But Daddy, Mama Patsy said I could be a flower girl and everything. We have to talk about it so I can tell Carrie Williams tomorrow at school."

Kenny lifted a brow at Patsy.

"I told her while she was in the bathtub," Patsy explained. "Don't you think it's a great idea?"

"Yeah, Daddy, don't you think it's a great idea?"

Kenny tugged on one of Wendy's braids. "It's a great idea, but not one we're going to discuss tonight."

"But Daddy—"

"No buts tonight, young lady." He leaned over and hugged her. "It's time for you to go to sleep."

"I'm not—"

Kenny cut her off with a familiar glare.

"Can we talk about it at breakfast?" She looked at Patsy. "You'll be here for breakfast, won't you, Mama Patsy?"

"Not in the morning, sweetheart. I'm going home tonight."

"Aren't you going to live here? With us?"

Patsy sat on the bed next to Wendy in response to the alarm she heard in the child's voice. She took Wendy's small hand in hers. "Of course I'm going to live here. But not until after the wedding."

"Why do you have to wait until the wedding? I want you to stay tonight."

Patsy shot Kenny a pleading glance.

"People don't live together until they're married, Peanut," he explained. "You know that."

"We're not married, Daddy, and we live together. Why can't Mama Patsy live here, too?"

Kenny couldn't argue with his daughter's reasoning. He thought he saw the makings of a fine attorney in her. "We live together because I'm the daddy and you're the daughter. That makes us a family. Mama Patsy won't be a member of the family until after the wedding."

"But Mama Patsy spent the night with us when we lived at the old house."

Yes, Kenny remembered, Patsy had stayed at the old house many nights when Leah was ill. She'd taken care of Wendy while he'd taken care of Leah. "That's different. Mama Patsy was Aunt Patsy then. Mommies and daddies don't live together until after they're married."

"But—"

"No more buts, young lady." He kissed her cheek and stood, motioning for Patsy to do the same. "We're going downstairs. Mama Patsy has to go home and you have to go to sleep."

She yawned. "Okay, Daddy. Sleep tight and don't let the bedbugs bite."

"We don't have bedbugs, Wendy," he and Patsy said at the same time. Wendy giggled, and he and Patsy shared a short laugh. Then Kenny switched off the light and left the room, closing the door behind him.

Again he placed his hand on Patsy's back, this time

to guide her down the steps. "She's something else, isn't she?" he asked.

Patsy stepped away from him. They'd been too close all day. Much too close. "I think I can navigate these steps on my own."

"What?"

Obviously, his touch did more to her than it did to him. "You don't have to guide me down the stairs."

"Oh," he said.

That was it? Well, if it meant nothing to him, it meant nothing to her. "Wendy is something else, all right. She's like her daddy," she said, answering his question. "All I can say is you're getting payback."

"Right..."

"Your mom and dad always said Wendy was as stubborn as you. Her questions and her protests are yours, Kenny. Don't try to deny it."

He grinned, then dropped down on the couch. "She is like me, isn't she?"

"Yes, she is. Including those cute little dimples."

"You know, Patsy, I don't think I'll ever get over it. She looks more like her mother than she does me, but I see so much of myself in her. Sometimes my heart aches with joy about that. And sometimes..."

His voice trailed off, so Patsy finished for him. "And sometimes it makes you feel sad that you couldn't see more of yourself in your parents."

He nodded, then clasped her hand in his. "I know my parents loved me. I know it and I always felt it. But a part of me always felt the difference in us."

"You were different," Patsy said lightly in an attempt to ease the tension of the moment.

"But there are two people out there somewhere that I look like. I may even have brothers and sisters."

"Why don't you try to find them, Kenny?" she asked, as she'd done many times before. "It's not too late."

He rubbed his thumb up and down her palm. "Maybe if I'd found out I was adopted while Leah and my parents were alive, but not now. Wendy has had too much pain and upheaval in her life. What she needs now is stability." He looked into Patsy's eyes, and her heartbeat speeded up. "She needs me. And she needs you."

"And that's why we're getting married—to give Wendy what she needs."

"Is that all, Patsy?" he asked, not taking his eyes from hers. "Is that going to be enough?"

"For now." The words came out a whisper.

He traced a finger down her jaw. "I do love you. You know that, don't you?"

Patsy's heart slammed against her chest. I do love you, he'd said. He'd said it before, but somehow tonight it sounded different. Oh, God, what was she thinking? Of course Kenny loved her. She was his best friend. "I know you love me, Kenny."

"Good," he said, his finger still tracing the lines of her face, leaving a trail of fire. "Do you know something else?"

"I love you, too."

His lips turned up in a smile. "Tell me something I don't know."

She took advantage of the levity of the moment and pushed away from him. "You've always been a smart mouth."

"Oh, no you don't," he said, pulling her back to him. "You didn't answer my question."

"What question?"

He rolled his eyes toward the ceiling. "Lord, please don't turn my best buddy into a ditsy wife."

She punched him in the shoulder. "Kenny!"

"You hit me a lot, you know. I hope you aren't going to be one of those women who beat their husbands."

She raised her chin a notch. "I don't know. That seems to be the best way to keep you in line."

"Well," he said, leaning his face close to hers, "I think I may have come up with a new way."

She put her hands on his chest. "Kenny..."

"Yes," he answered, and moved closer. She knew he was going to kiss her. She didn't want him to, she told herself, but then she remembered the kisses they'd shared earlier today. Yes, she did want him to kiss her.

"Did you know you nibble on your lower lip when you're nervous?"

"I do not."

He smiled and touched the corner of her lips. "You're doing it now. Are you nervous?"

She stopped nibbling on her lower lip. "Why should I be nervous?"

He lifted his shoulders, his hypnotic eyes fixed on hers, his finger massaging the corner of her lips. "I don't know. You tell me. Why are you nervous?"

"I'm not nervous."

He traced a finger across her lips and she trembled. "Maybe I'm wrong. Maybe you're not nervous."

Her hands tightened on his sweater and she realized she wanted to pull him to her. This couldn't happen. It was too fast. Much too fast. She jerked out of his embrace and jumped to her feet. "I've got to go, Kenny. I have some notes to go over for a meeting tomorrow." She grabbed her purse and her navy jacket and was out the door before he could say anything more.

Chapter Seven

Patsy could name two positive results of planning her wedding in a week's time. The first was the fun she and Wendy had doing girl things like trying on dresses. And the other was the fact that the planning kept her from spending a lot of time alone with Kenny.

Her attraction to him and his constant flirtation made her feel uncomfortable, unsteady, unsafe. And safety was one of the reasons she was marrying Kenny. "I don't need passion," she said aloud.

"What did you say, darling?" her mother asked.

Patsy turned and saw her mother standing in the kitchen doorway, her hands full of bags. The older woman was perfectly groomed as always, in her heels, hose and a figure-fitting, floral print dress. "I didn't hear you come in, Mama."

"I knocked, and when you didn't answer, I used my

key." She shifted the bags in her hands. "Now where do you want me to put these things?"

Patsy went to her mother and took a couple of the bags out her hands. "What is this, anyway?"

"Oh, this and that." Her mother followed her to the counter and set down her load.

Patsy quirked an eye at her. "This and that?"

"Yes, this and that. Now what were you saying when I walked in? Something about passion?"

"Oh, nothing," Patsy hedged, then went rummaging through the bags. "What is this, Mama?" she asked, holding up a flimsy, black lace bra and matching panties.

Her mother grabbed the garments and shoved them back in the bag. "Don't change the subject. You and Kenny aren't having problems in the bedroom, are you?"

"Mother, I don't believe you." Patsy thanked God for her dark skin. Without it, she'd be the proverbial blushing bride-to-be.

"Well, I wasn't born yesterday. I was married myself, remember?"

Actually, Patsy didn't remember the marriage. What she remembered was the divorce. "I was married once, too, Mama. And believe me, sex isn't everything."

"I won't disagree with you. Sex isn't everything, but sharing passion with a loving man is. Be glad that you and Kenny have it."

Patsy wanted to shout that she and Kenny didn't have it. They didn't even want it. "Kenny and I have friendship and respect for each other, Mama."

"Humph. Friendship and respect won't keep you warm on a cold night. Anyway, you're kidding yourself or trying to kid me when you say that's all there is between you and Kenny."

"That means you know more than I do."

"I always have," her mother said with a straight face. "I used to worry about you two. Remember that time Jimmy Jones caught you kissing? I knew that one day the two of you would start experimenting with sex."

Patsy smiled at the memory. All her young girlfriends had thought she was grown-up when they'd heard about the kiss. "That was kid stuff, Mama. Nothing ever happened between Kenny and me. So you worried for no reason."

"But something would have happened between you if Leah hadn't come along."

"That's a very big if, Mama."

"Oh, I don't know." Her mother brushed off the wrinkles the bags had made on her dress. "That's the past. Today's today. And in a couple of days you and Kenny are getting married. Who knows? Maybe this time next year I'll have another grandchild."

"Don't get your hopes up. Kenny and I aren't starting a family anytime soon."

"Well, you aren't getting any younger, Patsy. You need to have your first child before you're thirty-five. You know what the doctors say."

Patsy stood up. How had she allowed her mother to get her on the topic of babies? she wondered. "The doctors say women in good health can have babies into their late forties."

Her mother stood in turn and kissed her on the cheek. "Just make sure you don't try to set a record for being the oldest mother. Now, I've got to go. I promised my granddaughter a trip to the movies this afternoon. Do you want me to drive you over or are you meeting Kenny at the church?"

"I'm meeting him at the church. Thanks for keeping

Wendy this afternoon. We should pick her up early this evening.''

''No need to thank me. You know I love that little girl.'' She checked her watch. ''I really do have to go. I promised Kenny I'd pick her up before two.''

Patsy looked at the clock on the oven. ''I had no idea it was so late. I need to get a move on myself. I have to be at the florist in fifteen minutes. You and Wendy have fun,'' Patsy called, and rushed upstairs to get ready for her meeting with the florist and later with the minister. The former she didn't mind, but the latter scared her. She and Kenny had decided to tell the minister the truth about their marriage, and she wasn't sure what his response would be. What if he refused to perform the ceremony?

Well, she wouldn't think about that now. With the wedding only two days away, he *had* to do it. He had to.

Patsy opened her car door and got out as soon as she saw Kenny's car pull up behind her.

''Sorry I'm late,'' he said, running toward her. ''I lost track of time.''

''What were you doing?'' she asked, a bit irritated with him. What could be more important than their wedding?

He kissed her quickly on the lips and some of her irritation faded. Now she wanted to rest her head against his chest and have his strong arms hold her.

''What was that for?'' she asked, in an attempt to hide her response to the kiss.

''You were nibbling your lips again. I told you how you look when you do that.''

She lowered her eyes. She did remember. "Are you going to kiss me every time I nibble my lips?"

He grinned down at her. "That's my plan."

"I guess I'll have to stop doing it then," she said, and strode ahead of him to the church entrance.

It took Kenny a second or two to grasp what she'd said. When he did, he laughed and rushed to catch up with her. "Do you dislike my kisses that much?"

"Kenny," she warned. "Don't start with me on the church grounds."

Kenny lifted his arms in surrender. "Okay, wife." He opened the door for her and gave an exaggerated bow. "After you, milady."

Patsy rolled her eyes and brushed past him. "Stop playing, Kenny."

"Anything you say, dear," he said. "I'll be the perfect fiancé." He placed his hand against the base of her back.

"Kenny," she warned again.

"What did I do now? A guy can't even be a gentleman these days. What is the world coming to?"

Patsy moved to shake off his hand, but the minister entered the room. After he greeted them, he led them into his study.

"Well, well," he said. "Patsy and Kenny sittin' in a tree, *K-I-S-S-I-N-G.*"

Kenny laughed with the minister, and Patsy wanted to sink through the floor. She wondered if her mother and Reverend Wilkes had been discussing them.

"You two certainly have come a long way since those days."

"Thank God," Kenny added, and again he and the minister laughed. Patsy still didn't see what was so funny.

"So you two want to get married? I can't say I'm surprised. I had a feeling I'd marry the two of you one day."

"You already did," Patsy mumbled.

"That's right. First Kenny and Leah, then you and Theo. But marrying the two of you to each other is something I've always known would happen."

Well, you should have told me that before I married Theo, Patsy said to herself. It might have saved me a divorce.

"But marriage is serious business and your decision seems to have come quite quickly."

Kenny took Patsy's hand in his and linked their fingers, "We love each other."

"I know that, Kenny," the minister said. "But are you *in love* with each other?"

Kenny looked at Patsy while he reflected on the minister's question. "We love each other and we're committed to this marriage."

The pastor folded his hands in front of him. "Kenny, can you honestly say you love Patsy the way you loved Leah? And Patsy, do you love Kenny the way you loved Theo?"

Kenny tightened his hold on Patsy's hand and spoke first, this time looking at the minister. "I don't think I could love another woman the way I loved Leah. My love for her started in adolescence and grew with me into adulthood. There is a place in my heart that will always be hers. But that doesn't mean there isn't room to love Patsy just as much or just as well. Just not the same.

"Patsy is already a part of me. She has been for as long as I can remember. She's been my friend, my helper, my companion. I want her to be my wife, the mother of my daughter and of the children we'll have together. What I feel for her is forever—for richer, for poorer, in sickness and in health. It's already been proven.''

The minister kept his face clear of emotion and spoke to Patsy. "And how about you? Do you love Kenny the way you did Theo?"

Patsy knew tears were rolling down her cheeks from Kenny's words, and she prayed he wouldn't turn around and see them. "I agree with Kenny. I don't feel about him the way I did about Theo. What I have with Kenny makes me feel safe, protected. I know I can count on him. We've known each other for so long that I know I can depend on him. Our lives may change, but our trust will last. I'm sure of that."

As the minister looked back and forth between her and Kenny, Patsy took her free hand and wiped at the tears on her face. When the minister moved to offer her a tissue, she shook her head. He lifted a questioning brow, but desisted. Finally he nodded, with what Patsy hoped was his belief in the words they'd spoken. "But why now?"

"Reverend Wilkes," Patsy began. "You know Theo and I have been separated for two years. I'm not marrying Kenny on the rebound."

"But your divorce was final only recently. Are you sure you aren't rushing into this marriage to get over your divorce?"

Patsy shook her head. "I'm sure. The divorce becoming final gave me permission to get on with my life. I'm not marrying Kenny to save myself from the hurt of the past. I'm marrying him so that I can have a happy and fulfilling future."

"What about you, Kenny? I know Patsy was a great

help to you when Leah was ill. And I know she's been a godsend to you and little Wendy. Are you sure you're not using her to perform some role that you think needs filling in your household?''

Patsy held her breath while she waited for Kenny's answer.

''Kenny?'' the reverend prompted, when he didn't answer.

''Patsy's the first woman I've thought about since Leah died.''

Reverend Wilkes raised a skeptical brow at that statement.

''I'm not saying I haven't thought about a physical relationship with a woman,'' Kenny explained. ''I have. But the woman has never had a face until now. With Patsy. And with her it's not only physical. How could it be? She's already a part of my life.''

''And what about Wendy?''

''Sure, my concern for Wendy's welfare plays a role. She needs a mother, but I wouldn't marry anybody just to give her a mother. Wendy needs a stable and loving household, and I believe Patsy and I can give her that. I wouldn't marry Patsy if I didn't think that was true. I wouldn't risk the chance of bringing up my daughter in an unhappy home.''

The minister looked at each of them again. ''Do either of you have any questions?''

Kenny turned to Patsy. She shook her head. ''No, we don't have any questions,'' he answered.

Reverend Wilkes leaned back in his chair. ''I guess I'll see you on Saturday then.''

''Boy, that felt like one of Mrs. Miller's oral history tests,'' Kenny said once they were outside the church and next to their cars.

"A little."

"I liked what you said in there," Kenny confessed, showing a sudden interest in the tip of his black loafers.

She answered his unspoken question. "I meant it."

He looked up at her. "So did I."

She nodded. She'd known he'd meant it. She'd felt it.

"Do you want to go out for dinner or something?"

She did. "Don't you have to pick up Wendy?"

He gave a deep masculine grin that produced those too-sexy dimples. "I'm sure the baby-sitter can be convinced to keep her awhile longer."

"I think you're right." Patsy leaned toward him and kissed one of his dimples. It was the first time she'd voluntarily kissed him.

He stared at her lips after she'd stepped back from him, and she thought he wanted to kiss her again. She hoped he would. Disappointment washed over her when he opened her car door instead.

"We'll drop your car at your house and call your mother from there, all right?"

"Anything you say, husband."

Kenny willed his legs to take him to his car. He concentrated on his daughter to keep his thoughts and his body in check. It was no use. Between the words he and Patsy had spoken to Reverend Wilkes and her kiss just now, his body had reached its limit. He prayed he'd settle down by the time he reached Patsy's house.

Kenny and Patsy sittin' in a tree, K-I-S-S-I-N-G. He'd almost forgotten that. He and Patsy couldn't have been more than seven or eight at the time. It'd only been an experiment. Patsy's experiment. And he'd gone along with it, to his regret. Jimmy Jones had seen them, and soon everyone in town had known. The kiss had made Patsy a star among the girls and made him a big joke among the boys. But knowing that, even now, he'd do it all over again if she asked him. Patsy rarely asked for anything, so when she did he made sure she got what she wanted.

As they'd grown older, his role had turned to that of big brother. He wondered if she knew how many dates she hadn't gotten because of him. A word here and a word there, and the guys knew to back off. But old Theo had gotten through. Kenny still blamed himself for that. Sure, he'd told Patsy how he felt, but there must have been more he could have done. And talking to old Theo had been a waste. The guy's ego was bigger than the both of them.

So Patsy had married Theo. And that marked the one time Kenny hadn't given her what she wanted. He'd drawn the line at being "man of honor," choosing instead to be an usher. Theo hadn't thought much of Patsy's idea to make him a groomsman.

His and Patsy's wedding this Saturday would be the third wedding they'd been in together. Patsy had been a bridesmaid at his wedding, a year prior to him being an usher at hers. And this Saturday they were marrying each other.

The minister might not have been surprised by the news of their marriage, but Kenny sure as hell was. Surprised, but happy. And feeling very, very lucky. Unlike most men in most marriages— unlike him in his first— he knew what he was getting in Patsy and he knew what it took to make a marriage work. The former he'd learned the easy way, the latter the hard way.

He didn't want to think sad thoughts of the past tonight. No matter how hard he prayed or how much he wished, his failed first marriage couldn't be undone. He'd loved Leah as best he could, but it hadn't been enough. He would love Patsy enough, however. Of that he was certain.

Chapter Eight

"Thanks, Mrs. Mae." Kenny spoke into the wall phone in Patsy's kitchen. "Tell Wendy we'll pick her up tonight." He hung up the receiver and turned to Patsy. "Wendy didn't want to talk to me. She's making fudge with her grandma Mae. The little traitor."

"Be happy she likes her new grandmother," Patsy said, picking up her shoulder bag from the kitchen counter. "Things could be worse, you know."

Kenny leaned back against the counter and crossed his arms on his chest. "I *do* know and I *am* happy. Now, what do you want for dinner?"

Patsy thought he looked much too handsome in his black dress Dockers and black button-down shirt. It ought to be illegal for any man to have that much sex appeal. "Um, seafood," she said hesitantly, in answer to his question.

Kenny eased away from the counter and ambled over

to her. "Is that Boston Sea Party seafood, Red Lobster seafood or Po' Folks seafood?"

"Po' Folks," she said, fiddling with her bag. "Nobody makes better catfish."

"A woman after my own heart. You choose an eight-dollar meal at Po' Folks over a thirty-dollar meal at the Boston Sea Party. I'm going to have to keep a close watch on you or somebody might try to steal you away."

She looked at him. "Try to remember that fifteen years from now, when you're wondering why you married me."

"Won't happen, Patsy. Like I told the minister—better, worse. Richer, poorer. Old, young."

She stepped toward the foyer, glad she didn't have to stare into those dreamy brown eyes any longer. "I don't remember that old, young part."

"It's there. You just have to read between the lines."

She stared straight ahead as Kenny reached past her to open the front door. She didn't know where her bravado had gone. Where was the woman who had kissed him outside the church?

"What's on your mind?" Kenny asked, gently pushing the door closed again.

Why did he have to be so observant? she wondered. "I was thinking about the wedding," she said with a slight smile. "There are still a lot of details to work out, you know."

He shifted around so he could see her face. "What details? I thought everything was arranged."

"Almost," she said. "But there are still some things I need to do. I really ought to be taking care of some of those things tonight."

"Instead of going to dinner?"

She looked at him. "Would you mind? I really do

have things to do tonight. They slipped my mind with the church and all.''

Kenny understood what she meant about the church. The words they'd spoken had gotten to him, too. And then she'd kissed him. The first kiss she'd initiated. He'd felt like a real fiancé then. He shook his head. What was he thinking? He *was* a real fiancé. Tell yourself that's all you want, buster, he said silently, but you know better. "Would you rather pick up some takeout and bring it here?"

"Oh, Kenny, that would be better.... If you don't mind, that is.''

He couldn't very well tell her how disappointed he was, could he? No, he couldn't. If he told her, she'd force herself to go, and he didn't want her to do that. "No problem at all," he said, then moved to open the door again. "Look," he asked suddenly, "do you have work for me to do or will I be in the way if I stick around?"

"I don't have anything for you to do, but you're welcome to stay. If you want,'' she added.

He wanted, all right, but only if she wanted, too. "I'll be a sport about it this time. How about if we just take a raincheck for dinner? I figure you're entitled to a little time alone before our wedding.''

She leaned over and kissed him on his strong jaw. "Oh, Kenny, I'm so glad you understand. Today has been an emotional roller coaster. I didn't realize how much that visit to the church had taken out of me.''

He placed a hand on her cheek, resisting the temptation to caress her soft skin. "I always understand you, Patsy.''

"You do, don't you?''

He dropped his hand and finally pulled open the front

door. "I'd better get out of here before I change my mind."

She looked at him and thought she saw something akin to banked passion in his eyes. She blinked, and when she opened her eyes, the teasing glint was back. "Give Wendy a big good-night kiss for me and tell Mama I'll call her in the morning."

"Okay," he said, thinking how quickly his plans for the evening had gone down the drain. He turned and headed toward his car.

He wanted to be with Patsy tonight, to hold on to what they'd shared at the church. But Patsy, in typical fashion, wanted to analyze it. He understood her, but he was learning how much she could irritate him. With that thought, he backed out of the driveway and headed for Mrs. Mae's house. Hopefully, she and Wendy wouldn't mind spending the evening with him.

Patsy lay awake and watched the second hand on the clock on her nightstand pass twelve again. When she'd awakened at about three in the morning, she'd chosen to count the number of times the hand passed twelve instead of counting sheep. She probably should've stuck with sheep, because counting second-hand revolutions hadn't worked. It was now two minutes before her alarm was due to go off. Almost eight o'clock. And she hadn't been back to sleep. She'd been staring at the clock for almost five hours, though she'd stopped counting revolutions after the first half hour and allowed her mind to focus on the wedding this afternoon. Her wedding.

Today was her wedding day. She pressed the alarm off right before the second hand hit eight o'clock. Soon her mother, Wendy and Marilyn would arrive and they'd begin preparing for the big event. At least her mother and Marilyn would let her help today. Last night, when they'd decorated Kenny's house for the ceremony, they'd forbidden her to even think about helping them, but they'd allowed Kenny and Derrick to help.

"You did all the planning, so Kenny can do all the work," her mother had said. And that's the way it had gone. Patsy had seen Kenny for only a few minutes. He'd been too busy to do more than give her a quick hello and an even quicker kiss on the cheek. They'd all been busy, and she'd been left alone with her thoughts.

Patsy tossed back the comforter and eased out of bed. That was her problem—she thought too much. She covered her face with both hands, yawned, then dropped her arms to her sides and walked to the windows facing the street. She pulled back the curtains and looked out on the morning. The clear sky bespoke a beautiful day. A perfect day for a wedding.

Seeing her mother drive up, she dropped the curtain and grabbed her robe off the foot of the bed. She met Wendy at the bottom of the stairs. Patsy recognized the denim jumper and pink pullover Wendy wore as the outfit she'd given the child earlier in the year.

"Good morning, sweetheart," she said to the little girl before kissing her on the forehead. "I bet you're tired."

"We're tired," Marilyn said, entering the door with an armful of packages. "She's excited. She can't do anything but talk about the wedding."

Patsy smiled down at Wendy and saw the excitement sparkling in her young eyes. "Are you ready for the big event?"

Wendy bobbed her head. "My dress is so pretty, Mama Patsy. Can I put it on now?"

Patsy laughed. "Not yet, sweetheart. We don't want to get all wrinkled before the wedding."

"I won't get wrinkled," the little girl promised. "I'll sit real still."

Patsy's mother entered the house last. "No, you won't, Wendy. Did you forget your promise to help me with the corsages and boutonnieres?"

Wendy's lips formed an O that revealed she'd indeed forgotten.

"Well, why don't you follow me into the kitchen so we can make breakfast for Mama Patsy and Miss Marilyn?" Patsy's mother suggested.

Patsy's eyes followed her mother and Wendy as they made their way to the kitchen, the six-year-old chattering all the way.

"How you holding up, girl?" Marilyn asked.

Patsy grimaced. "Don't ask."

"You're not getting cold feet, are you?"

Patsy shook her head. Her problem wasn't cold feet; more like hot heart.

"What is it then?"

Patsy glanced toward the kitchen. "Let's go upstairs."

Marilyn followed Patsy to her bedroom, where they sat on her bed. "Now spill it," she said.

"I'm starting to *feel* things," Patsy began.

Marilyn leaned closer. "What kind of things?"

Patsy stood up and paced. "Things about Kenny. And me."

"Well, I hate to say it, but I told you so."

Patsy stopped pacing and glared at Marilyn. "You're not helping."

"Sorry," her friend said, but her voice held no conviction. "Go on."

Patsy resumed her pacing. "It's moving too fast. We

were supposed to be established in our marriage before we had these feelings."

Marilyn crossed her denim-clad legs and begin swinging her sandaled foot back and forth. "I don't see what you're complaining about. You love him already. The feelings are natural."

"You don't understand," Patsy said, and dropped facedown on the bed.

"You're right. I don't understand a woman who's upset because she has feelings for her husband-to-be." Marilyn paused. "Unless the husband-to-be doesn't have feelings for her. Is that it?"

"I wish," Patsy mumbled into the bedcovers. That was the other part of the problem. Kenny was having feelings, too.

"What? I can't understand you."

"I'm not the only one with these feelings," Patsy repeated, louder this time.

"Well, I told you so."

Patsy lifted her head and squinted in Marilyn's direction. "You might as well be downstairs helping Mama and Wendy fix breakfast for all the help you are."

Her friend propped her elbow on her crossed legs and rested her chin in her open palm. "What do you want me to do? Feel sorry for you because you want your husband and he wants you? I don't get it."

"It's too much like it was with Theo."

"Whoa, there," Marilyn ordered. "Kenny is not Theo. And he's nothing like Theo."

"I know that," Patsy said. And she did know it in her head. Her heart, though, was another matter. "But the feelings remind me of Theo. Our relationship was so intense in the beginning. Too intense. And look what happened to us."

"Don't start comparing your marriage to Kenny with your marriage to Theo. You're asking for problems if you do."

"I know, I know," Patsy said. "But I can't stop myself. I'm so afraid."

"Afraid of what? Afraid you're actually in love with your husband?"

Patsy shook her head. "Afraid these feelings will get in the way of our developing a strong marriage. It's happening too fast, Marilyn. Less than two weeks ago, Kenny and I were buddies. And now we're kissing and thinking about what those kisses could lead to. We were supposed to get married and then let nature take its course."

"Breakfast's ready," Patsy's mother called from downstairs.

Marilyn uncrossed her legs and stood up. "Maybe nature *is* taking its course. It's just not the course you planned." With that, she opened the bedroom door and left Patsy staring after her.

"It's only a wedding," Kenny told himself as he adjusted his bow tie in his bedroom mirror. But he knew it wasn't only a wedding. It was his second marriage. When he'd married Leah, he'd been young and full of love and the lust that had so tightly attached itself to that love.

The bedroom door opened and Derrick walked in. "Ready, old man?" he asked.

Kenny pulled at his gray cutaway coat until it felt comfortable across his broad shoulders. "About as ready as I'm going to get. Is Patsy here yet?"

Derrick nodded. "She's beautiful, man. And so are

her mother and Wendy. Marilyn's looking good enough to eat. Do you know if she's dating anybody?''

"Who? Patsy's mother or Wendy?"

"All right, Mr. Smart Pants, you know I'm talking about Marilyn. That woman is gorgeous. Why haven't I noticed her before?"

Kenny snorted. "Probably because the beautiful women worshipping at your feet blocked your view."

"No need to get ugly, old pal. I just want to know the lay of the land, so to speak, where Marilyn is concerned."

"Come off it, man. You need another woman hanging on to you like I need another head. What would you do with her?"

Derrick merely grinned. "I'm sure I'd think of something."

Kenny didn't bother to comment on that statement. "You need to find yourself one woman and settle down. That is, if you can find a woman who can tame you."

Derrick pushed Kenny away from the mirror and adjusted his own coat. "Not bad," he said, after studying his profile.

"Maybe you're not married because you don't want to share your mirror," Kenny offered, but he knew that wasn't the reason. Derrick wasn't married because he hadn't found a need to be married. Having too many women spoiled a man that way.

"Marriage is for men like you, Sanders."

"Men like me? Now what's that supposed to mean?"

Derrick walked away from the mirror and patted his pocket, checking for the ring box Kenny had given him earlier. "Are you ready?"

"As soon as you answer my question. What do you mean by 'men like me'?"

"Men content to settle for one rose. Men like me want to sample the whole garden."

"That's what you say now. But you'll find a woman who'll make you forget there is a garden." That's what Leah had done for him. She'd made him forget all women. Until now. Until Patsy. Strange that a woman he'd known and loved all his life had been the one to awaken desires he'd packed away when he lost Leah.

"You think so, huh?" Derrick asked, breaking into his thoughts.

"Yeah, I do."

Derrick opened the bedroom door. "It's time, man." He clapped Kenny on the back. "Let's do it."

Kenny stepped out of the room in front of Derrick. In less than thirty minutes he'd be a married man. Again. He couldn't wait.

Kenny barely noticed Marilyn when she entered the decorated living room and made her way to the arch that separated the bridal party from the guests. His eyes waited for his bride. A smile touched his lips when Wendy came through the door, lovely in her pink lace gown. She appeared nervous as she entered the room, but when her eyes met his, her shoulders straightened and her smile appeared. She tossed her flower petals with gusto.

Kenny felt the quickening of his pulse as he waited for Patsy. When she finally entered the room, his knees went weak.

"Told you she was gorgeous," Derrick whispered.

Kenny didn't respond. He couldn't. He didn't think his lips would move. Patsy was more than beautiful. She was a vision of life and loveliness. The pale pink and white gown, unlike any wedding dress he'd ever seen, outlined her every curve. This wasn't the wedding gown of a virgin, this was the wedding gown of a sensuous woman. His woman. Soon to be his wife.

When she reached him, he thought he saw tears in her eyes, but he couldn't be sure because of her veil. He took her gloved hand in his and they faced the minister.

Somehow he was able to say "I do" at the right time. When it was Patsy's turn, he felt her tremble, then give her own soft responses.

He didn't hear anything else until the minister asked for the rings. When Kenny placed his ring on Patsy's finger and pledged his love to her, she trembled again. More than anything he wanted to pull her into his arms and reassure her.

Next, Patsy placed her ring on his finger. She lifted her eyes to him and he saw the tears clearly. They caused his heart to pound faster and harder. Her pledge of love almost caused tears to form in his eyes.

Kenny didn't hesitate when the minister finally gave him permission to kiss his bride. He lifted her veil and took her face in both his hands, using his thumbs to wipe away her tears. When she gave him a weak smile, he lowered his head and captured her lips with his own. He'd planned to give her a chaste kiss, but sometimes events take on a life of their own. The kiss was one of those events.

When she groaned in her throat and placed her hands against his shirt, he thought he'd die if he didn't have her right now. He deepened the kiss, taking advantage as she so sweetly opened her mouth.

He felt a hand on his shoulder before he heard the minister's exaggerated cough. Though it pained him to do so, he lifted his mouth from Patsy's. She kept looking up at him, her hands still resting on his chest, her lips

slightly swollen from his kiss. More than anything, he
wanted to kiss her again. He leaned his head down to
hers once more, but Derrick and the guests started clapping, and Patsy dropped her hands from his chest. He
had no choice but to raise his head, take her hand in his
and face the small group.

"We're married now, Daddy," he heard Wendy say.

He looked down at her and winked. "You bet we are,
Peanut. You bet we are."

Chapter Nine

Patsy nibbled at her lower lip while she and Kenny stood in the front door and waved after Wendy and Leah's parents. She'd made it through the reception on a prayer, but if Kenny didn't take his hands off her waist soon, she knew she'd shatter into a million pieces.

"Well," he said, after closing the door, "we made it. How does it feel, Mrs. Sanders?"

Scary. "I don't know. How does it feel to have a new wife?"

He draped an arm around her shoulder, and the relief she'd felt for the mere second when he'd removed his hand from her waist fled. "It feels great. Let's have another drink. I want to make a private toast."

The heat from Kenny's arm scorched her bare skin. For the hundredth time that day she wished she'd chosen a wedding dress that covered her shoulders. Maybe the heat wouldn't be so bad if there was material separating his skin from hers. But she hadn't been able to resist the pale pink off-the-shoulder gown with its white lace bodice. Nor the chic matching white hat that had anchored her veil. Her mother, Marilyn and Wendy had loved the bridal ensemble, too.

Kenny positioned her under the arch. "Don't move. I'll be right back."

And he was. With glasses of champagne for both of them. He handed her a glass and lifted his to her.

"To my wife, Patsy Sanders, the woman I've chosen to share the rest of my days. May your years with me be the happiest ones of your life. I promise to honor you and protect you and keep you safe as long as I live. Thank you for agreeing to become my wife."

He clinked his glass to hers, then drank quickly, while she did the same. Then he took her glass and placed it, along with his, on the mantle over the fireplace. "Now come here," he said, when he turned around. "We have some unfinished business."

Patsy didn't listen to the protests that sprang up in her heart. What was the sense in denying that she wanted this as much, if not more, than Kenny did? So when he opened his arms, she walked freely and hopefully into them.

His arms tightened around her, and he pulled her so close she felt as if she'd be sucked right into his body. She didn't protest, because she wanted to be as close as she could get. Her mouth opened automatically when his head descended and his lips touched hers. Nothing about this kiss was tame. It didn't have to deepen; it started deep. It didn't have to ask for entrance; entrance had already been granted. It met no resistance. What was the point of useless protests?

Patsy gave herself to the moment. All she thought

about was Kenny. Her hands tightened on his shirtfront before relaxing and sliding up his chest and around his neck. She sighed and gave herself to her husband.

Kenny felt Patsy's immediate surrender, and it raised his ardor as nothing else could. She opened to him like a flower in the rain. And he savored her for the natural beauty and wonder that was her. This was Patsy. His Patsy. His friend. His wife.

When she slipped her arms around his neck, he lifted her off the floor so he could feel her breasts pressed against his chest. His hands caressed her waist and her back, holding her tight against him. But it wasn't enough. He still couldn't get as close as he wanted to. He couldn't touch her the way he wanted. The kiss she returned required more of him than he could give in their present position.

Without taking his lips from hers and without lowering her feet to the floor, he moved slowly to the couch and sat down, dragging Patsy onto his lap. Now he had the access he craved. He raised his hands to her bare shoulders and caressed her silken, ebony skin. Her whimper encouraged him, and he allowed his hands to slip down the bodice of her gown. He ached to touch the full breasts that pressed so enticingly against him.

He gasped when his fingers touched the tip of her breast. This was what he wanted. What he needed. Patsy moaned as his fingers tweaked her already erect nipple. The grainy sensation of the nipple against his fingers, coupled with her sensuous moaning, almost sent him over the edge.

He lifted his mouth from hers slightly and whispered, "Let's go upstairs."

Patsy's unfocused eyes sharpened slightly, then widened. Before he knew what was happening, she pulled away from him.

"What's wrong?" he asked, still in a sensual haze. He wanted her. Now.

"What are we doing, Kenny?"

He leaned over and pulled her back to him. "I think we're in trouble if you don't know."

He felt her hands at his chest again, but something was different. This time her hands were pushing him away, not pulling him to her. He lifted his head from hers.

"What's the matter?" he asked, his heart pounding with need.

Patsy's breasts still tingled from Kenny's touch, but she had to put a stop to what they were doing before it went too far. "What are we up to, Kenny?" she asked again.

"I think we're about to make love," he said calmly.

"But why?"

"Because we want each other," he offered. "I know I want you and I think you want me."

"But it's too soon. I'm not ready yet."

Kenny grinned. "I hate to disagree with you on our wedding day, sweetheart, but I think you *are* ready." He moved closer to her. "More than ready."

Patsy scooted back on the couch and put her hand out to keep him away. "My body is ready, Kenny, but my mind isn't."

He stared at her as if she were speaking a foreign language. "What?"

She gathered her dress in her hands and stood up. "You heard me. My body is ready, but my mind isn't. I need more time before we make love."

"Sweetheart—" he began, but she cut him off.

"You promised, Kenny. You said we'd wait until I'm ready. Well, I'm not."

"You're not ready," he repeated, as if not believing her words. "Then what just happened between us?"

"Our bodies got a little ahead of our brains," she explained.

Kenny's eyes caressed her face, and she felt it as potently as if he'd kissed her.

"Speak for yourself, sweetheart," he said. "My head and my body were on the same path."

"Oh." She wished for something better to say, but nothing came to her.

"Yes. 'Oh,'" he said. "But your head and your body were in different places. That's what you're telling me?"

"I knew you'd understand."

He nodded, his passion-filled gaze telling her he understood, but that he didn't like it.

"We talked about this, Kenny," she repeated. "It was your idea."

"I know, I know," he said. "You don't have to repeat my own words to me."

"But you were right then and you're right now. What would it accomplish if we fell into bed?"

His burning gaze told her she didn't want him to answer that question.

"I know what it would accomplish," she answered for him. "Nothing."

Kenny raised a skeptical brow. "Nothing?" He could think of a few things.

"Nothing positive. It would only confuse us. Trust me, Kenny. Sex can become a crutch, and I don't want that again."

He swore softly. "And you think I do?"

"Don't you see that going to bed together now would

only make it that much harder to get past the sex? To base our marriage on things other than sex?''

He didn't answer, and she knew he was angry. She also knew he'd get over it. "I guess I'd better get out of this dress," she said.

Kenny stared up at her, the flames of passion still burning in his eyes for her to see. "I guess you'd better."

Patsy turned quickly, not trusting herself to stay any longer, and almost ran up the stairs to the room she'd chosen for herself. Of the two available rooms—one next to Wendy's room, the other next to Kenny's—she'd chosen the former. She'd ignored the voice in the back of her mind that told her she was using Wendy as a shield against her own weakness, and she hid behind the weak excuse that she liked being at the front of the house.

As she stood in the middle of her room now, she knew it would be a shield only if Kenny allowed it to be. He'd barreled through her resistance tonight as surely as if he'd barreled through the walls separating their rooms. Any protection she had against her rising passion was a gift from him.

She turned to her full-length mirror, one of the few pieces of her furniture that had already been moved to Kenny's house...now her home. Her fingers touched her well-kissed lips, then traced along the path of heat he'd left on her shoulders and chest. She stopped short of touching her breasts as he'd done and fell back on the bed.

What have I gotten myself into? she wondered, staring at the ceiling.

Kenny sat on the couch, where only a few precious minutes ago he'd held fulfillment in his arms, and practiced taking deep breaths. Too bad they weren't helping. He shifted in his seat and adjusted his pants. That didn't help, either. What he needed was to get Patsy out of his thoughts. He shook his head. What he needed, he corrected, was to get Patsy in his bed, where she belonged. She was his wife, for God's sake.

You asked for this, buddy, he reminded himself. Derrick called you a fool and he was right.

Kenny propped his shoe-clad feet on the table in front of him and wondered what had possessed him to tell Patsy they'd wait to live as man and wife. What in the hell had he been thinking?

He'd been thinking he could control his attraction for her. But he'd been wrong. There was no controlling his attraction. It was there. And it was alive. And it needed to be fed. Soon.

"Damn Theo Baxter," Kenny said, then choked out a tired laugh. He didn't know why he blamed Theo. If the guy had been any kind of man, he and Patsy would still be married and there'd be no Patsy Sanders.

"The hell with it," he said, then got up and grabbed the champagne bottle and a glass and made his way up the stairs. He walked to his bedroom, then turned and stared at Patsy's door.

He knew if he knocked, she'd let him in. And if she let him in, he'd be in her bed within seconds. Her body wanted his as much as his wanted hers. Her mind was another matter. He shook his head slowly. That analytical mind of hers was giving him the first sleepless night of his new marriage.

With a sigh, he turned and entered his room, closing his door on the heaven he knew he'd find in her arms.

* * *

Patsy woke early the next morning, refreshed from a much-needed night of peaceful sleep. When she looked at her face in her bathroom mirror, she decided lack of sleep had been her downfall last night. If she hadn't been so tired from all the wedding plans and all the worrying, her resistance wouldn't have been so low and she would have been better able to control her emotions...and things wouldn't have gotten so out of hand with Kenny.

Well, she thought, today is a new day. We can't change yesterday but today we can start anew. With that thought in mind, she quickly showered and dressed so she could go downstairs and prepare breakfast.

Twenty-five minutes later, she stood in her new kitchen mixing pancake batter and humming her personal rendition of the wedding march.

"What are you doing?"

She turned from her batter and saw Kenny leaning against the doorjamb. She willed her eyes not to dwell on his broad, bare chest or the flat stomach exposed by the pajama bottoms riding low on his hips. "Fixing breakfast. What does it look like I'm doing?"

He pushed away from the door jamb and ambled over to the garbage can in the corner. She thought she saw him deposit an empty bottle. An empty champagne bottle. Had he drunk all that?

He turned to her. "No, I didn't drink it," he answered, as if he'd heard her question. "But I seriously thought about it."

"Well, then." Remembering that this was a new day and that she was in control, Patsy decided to direct their conversation to a safer topic. "You can set the table. The pancakes should be ready in a few minutes."

Kenny strode lazily to the cabinets and pulled out the

required place settings. "You didn't have to cook breakfast. I'm used to cooking every morning, so I might as well keep at it."

"I know I don't have to do it," she said, pouring the pancake mix on the griddle, her back to him. "I want to. I need to help out around here. It's my home now, too."

Kenny opened the refrigerator and removed the gallon jug of orange juice. He filled two glasses, then turned and handed her one. "Right. It's your home. You're not a servant."

Patsy silently counted to ten. She knew Kenny was spoiling for an argument, but she wasn't going to give him one. She was in control. "I know I'm not a servant, Kenny," she said calmly. "But since I live here, it's only fair that I share in the work."

He opened his mouth as if to offer further protest, but he didn't. "Okay, we'll share the job then. I'll cook some mornings and you can cook others."

"Deal," she said, then lifted her glass of orange juice to him to seal the compromise.

Kenny pulled a chair from the table and sprawled out in it, his long legs spread wide. Patsy turned back to the griddle.

"What do you plan to do today?" he asked.

"I need to pick up some more of my things from the house. Most of them are already packed, but there are still a few more items to take care of."

Kenny chugalugged the last of his juice. "No problem. Derrick said he'd come by and help. I'll drive the truck and we'll have everything loaded before you know it."

"Good. Marilyn said she'd drop by, too. With the four of us, we should be done in no time."

Kenny nodded. "Did you notice that Derrick and Marilyn left the reception together yesterday?"

She'd noticed, but Kenny's closeness had kept the thought from working its way to the front of her mind. "That's another reason I'm glad she's dropping by the house. I can't wait to hear what happened. Can you imagine her and Derrick together?"

"I was a bit skeptical when he asked me about her, but who knows, maybe she's exactly what he needs."

"He asked you about her? What did he say?"

Kenny laughed. "Who's the attorney here?" he asked. "He wanted to know if she was seeing anyone special, that's all."

"Marilyn's very attractive, but she's certainly not like the women Derek normally dates. He seems to like a little more flash than substance."

Her observation made Kenny smile. Flashy did describe the women Derrick dated. "We'll have to wait and see what happens then, won't we?"

"You talk to Derrick and I'll talk to Marilyn, then later we can compare notes."

Kenny laughed again. "When did you become such a busybody?"

"I'm not a busybody. I'm interested in our friends. Wouldn't it be great if they fell in love and got married?"

Kenny shook his head, taking pleasure in this romantic side of Patsy. His eyes traveled from her plain gold necklace down the buttons of her white cotton blouse, which pulled tight across her full breasts, to the belt buckle at her trim waist and down... No, he told himself, don't think about what's inside those faded jeans. He forced his eyes back to her face, and what he saw told him she knew where his thoughts had been. He didn't try to deny it. "What did you think of Mrs. Walden, Wendy's teacher?"

"She seemed nice enough," Patsy said, the relief in her eyes plain for him to see. She turned back to the stove.

"But?"

Patsy brought the platter of pancakes to the table along with the bacon. After she sat down, she said, "I don't know. There was something familiar about her. Like I knew her from somewhere. I can't explain it."

"I know what you mean. I had that same feeling of familiarity. Where's she from?"

"I don't know. I asked her, but I don't remember her answer. I think someone interrupted us before she told me."

Kenny nodded and began to dig into his breakfast. "Your father seemed to enjoy himself. He and your mother spent most of the reception together."

Patsy grimaced. "I noticed."

"You have a problem with that?"

She lifted her shoulders slightly. She'd felt sadness at seeing her mother and father together. "Not really. I just don't want Mama to get hurt again."

"They're both older and wiser now. Maybe they'll find their way back together."

Patsy poured more syrup on her pancakes. She refused to be drawn into that line of thinking. She'd spent most of her childhood wishing for her parents to get back together. She wasn't going to start doing it again. "Whatever. Anyway, I'm not borrowing trouble. It's Mama's life. And like you said, they're both adults."

Kenny didn't respond, so they ate the rest of their breakfast in comfortable silence. Finally, Kenny pushed his plate away. "That was good. Maybe you *should* cook breakfast everyday."

"Too late, buster. You volunteered and I'm not letting you out now." Patsy wiped her mouth with the cloth napkin Kenny had placed next to her plate. "And to let you know how good a sport I am, I'll let you do the cleanup this morning."

"Where are you going?" he asked, when she pushed her chair back from the table.

She stood and placed her hands on the back of her vacated chair. "I have a couple of errands to run. I'll meet you at my house in about an hour and a half."

"Errands to run?"

"What can I say? You married a busy woman."

Chapter Ten

Patsy pushed her chair back from the table. "Everyone for dessert?" she asked cheerfully, hoping some of her cheeriness would rub on their sullen guests. Marilyn and Derrick hadn't said more than ten words to each other all day. They didn't fool Patsy, though. She'd seen the sly glances Derrick had sent Marilyn as well as the ones she'd sneaked of him.

"None for me," Derrick said, with another quick glance across the table at Marilyn. "I have to go."

Patsy put a hand on his chair to keep him seated. "You can't go yet. You've got to eat some of Kenny's cheesecake. It's the best."

"No, really..." Derrick began, this time looking at his watch.

"Kenny'll be insulted if you don't stay," Patsy said, shooting a pointed look across the table at Kenny.

He sat up straighter in his chair. "I sure will be, man. I made it especially for today."

Patsy picked up her plate and reached for Marilyn's.

"Let me help, Patsy," Marilyn offered.

Patsy forced herself not to respond to the plea in her friend's eyes. It didn't take a genius to figure out that Marilyn would do about anything to get out of this room.

"No, you won't. You'll sit right where you are." She shot Kenny another glance. "Kenny'll help me. Won't you, Kenny?"

"Sure," he said, taking his plate and reaching for Derrick's.

"We'll be back in a minute," Patsy said, then left the room, with Kenny following after her.

When the door between the kitchen and the dining room closed, Kenny asked, "What do you think you're doing? Can't you see those two are in misery?"

"Keep your voice down," Patsy whispered. She peeked out the door and saw Marilyn and Derrick looking everywhere but at each other.

Kenny stood behind her and gazed over her head. "Are they fighting yet?"

"Worse. They're pretending the other doesn't exist."

"I wonder what happened last night," Kenny said.

Patsy closed the door and went to the refrigerator for the cheesecake. "I asked Marilyn, but she acted like she didn't know what I was talking about."

Kenny handed her four dessert plates from the cabinet. "Derrick wasn't much better. All he said was, 'You don't want to know.'"

"But I *do* want to know."

Kenny stepped behind her and put his hands around her small waist. He rested his chin on the top of her head. "You are one nosy woman. Did you know that?"

"Concerned," she corrected. "Not nosy." Her hands trembled as she continued to dish out the cheesecake. Thanks to Marilyn and Derrick, she'd managed to keep away from Kenny all day and now here she was, trapped in his arms in her own kitchen. Their kitchen.

She turned in his embrace. "Take this out there before our friends decide to leave."

Kenny backed away from her and rested against the counter behind him. "No one would ever guess this was our honeymoon. You're more concerned with Derrick and Marilyn than you are with me. If I didn't know better, I'd think you were keeping them here so we wouldn't have to be alone."

"Don't be silly," she said, hating that once again he'd read her thoughts and intentions with precision. "Now are you going to help me take these plates out there or not?"

He gave her a lazy grin. "I'll help, but you can't keep them here all night, Patsy. They have to go home sometime."

Fifteen minutes later, Patsy knew he was right.

"That's it for me, guys," Derrick said. "I have to leave."

"Me, too," Marilyn added.

Patsy stood because they did. "There's no need to rush. The evening's still young."

Derrick cast a knowing glance at Kenny. "You guys are having the weirdest honeymoon I've ever heard of. You can bet I wouldn't be hosting dinner parties if I'd just got married."

"You'll probably never have a honeymoon," Marilyn mumbled.

Patsy sucked in her breath when Derrick opened his

mouth to respond to her friend's comment. Relief flooded through her when he smiled instead.

"I'll talk to you two next week. After the honeymoon," he clarified, then kissed Patsy on her forehead before shaking Kenny's hand.

She and Marilyn walked ahead of the two men to the door. "What was that all about?" Patsy whispered to Marilyn.

"Nothing," Marilyn said before giving her a brief hug and opening the door. "I'll call you next week."

Patsy peeked out the side panel and watched the two of them walk to their vehicles. She saw Derrick stop at Marilyn's car and say something to her. Marilyn shook her head and hurriedly got into her vehicle. Derrick said something else, then threw up his hands. He marched to his motorcycle, strapped on his helmet, revved his engine, then spun out of the driveway.

Patsy turned to Kenny, who was standing behind her. "I guess he was a tad upset."

"Some women know exactly which buttons to push to upset a man. Some have even turned it into an art form."

Patsy thanked God again for her dark skin. Keeping her pique in check, she asked, "How would you know? If my calculations are correct, your experience with women is somewhat limited." She left Kenny standing in the foyer with his mouth open.

After Patsy's crack about his limited experience with women, Kenny had gone to bed plotting devious ways to upset her equilibrium. But now, as he looked at himself in the fresh light of morning, he didn't like what he saw. What had he been doing? What had he been thinking?

Patsy was his best friend, and all he could think about was getting her into bed. He'd promised to give her time to grow in their marriage, yet he'd gone back on that promise on their wedding night. He'd pushed. And continued pushing. Well, today was a new day. Today he'd make up for his childish behavior. And he'd start with breakfast.

The phone rang when he was setting the table.

"Hi, Daddy, guess who this is?"

Kenny's spirits lifted at the sound of his daughter's happy voice. "Whitney Houston?"

She giggled, and the sound was a balm to his aching heart. "No, not Whitney Houston."

He named a few more people before she took pity on him. "I fooled you, Daddy," she said, then giggled again. "It's me. Wendy."

"Wendy? Wendy who?"

He heard her speak to her grandparents. "Daddy doesn't know who I am."

"Wendy Sanders, Daddy," she said to him.

"This couldn't be my Wendy Sanders. You sound too grown-up to be my Wendy."

"My birthday is Saturday. I'll be seven years old."

"Well, that explains why I didn't know who you were. You're older than you were when you left."

"Where's Mama Patsy, Daddy? I want to say hi to her."

"Hold on a minute, Peanut. I'll get her."

Kenny placed the receiver on the counter and left the kitchen to get Patsy. He met her coming down the stairs. "Wendy's on the phone. She wants to talk to you."

Patsy ran to the extension in the foyer. "Wendy, sweetheart, I miss you. Are you having fun?"

Kenny couldn't hold back his smile, nor could he

deny the joy he felt hearing Patsy talk to Wendy. He knew he should go and hang up the kitchen extension, but he couldn't take his eyes off his wife. She wore jeans again, so she looked terrific, but that wasn't it. This morning she was peaceful, relaxed, comfortable. Comfortable, as if she'd always lived here with him.

Patsy laughed. "You did, did you? Well, I wish I was there with you. I haven't been to Disney World in a long time...

"No, no. I can't come down there now. You have fun with your grandparents and hurry home. Your daddy and I miss you....

"Okay, sweetheart," Patsy said, nodding her head. "Let me give the phone back to your daddy.... I know, sweetheart, I love you, too."

Patsy handed the phone to Kenny, and he noticed the tears in her eyes.

Wendy proceeded to tell Kenny everything she'd done yesterday and everything she planned to do today. When she wound down, he said, "Tell your grandparents hello for me, Peanut. And hurry home. I don't want you all grown up when you get back here on Saturday."

Wendy giggled. "Okay, Daddy, and don't forget my birthday party."

He looked at Patsy and grinned. "We won't forget your party, Peanut. I promise. Okay, bye-bye, now."

Kenny hung up the phone. "She's really something, isn't she?"

"She's been gone only a couple of days and already I miss her so much. I'll be glad when she gets back."

Kenny raised a skeptical brow. "You know she's going to run us ragged, don't you?"

"Of course. But I can't wait. I love it."

"And she loves you."

Patsy grinned, and something inside him softened. "I know and I love that, too. You know, we have to get started on her party."

"There isn't much left to do," Kenny said. "I talked to the parents of most of her friends last week. And I got Wendy to help with the invitations before she left. I even hired a clown. All we have to do is decorate the house and buy the cake."

"You think you're good, don't you?" Patsy teased.

Kenny rubbed his knuckles against the front of his shirt. "Some of us are like that."

"You almost have me believing that load of baloney," she said, then punched him in the shoulder. "Anyway, you've done good."

Kenny rubbed his shoulder. "Well, thank you very much, Mrs. Sanders. Remind me to show you another way to demonstrate your appreciation."

Kenny saw the light in Patsy's eyes dim and cursed himself for the sexual innuendo. He draped an arm around her shoulders and guided her to the kitchen. "I didn't mean anything by that. Now come on and eat the fabulous breakfast I've prepared."

Kenny managed to get their conversation back to the light tone it had had before his sexual comment, and they were able to enjoy a pleasant breakfast. After they'd eaten and cleared the table, he asked, "Why don't we do a Wendy activity today? Something fun. Like we used to do when we were kids."

"I don't know about that. We'd probably get in trouble for sneaking into the movies."

Kenny laughed. They'd only done that once and they'd gotten caught even then. "Nothing like that. How about we spend the day in the park? We can go bike riding, paddleboating, anything you want to do."

Patsy studied Kenny's face. "You're serious, aren't you?"

He tapped her on the nose. "Very serious. We were supposed to use this week to get accustomed to living together and to firm up the foundation of our marriage. I can't think of a better way than spending a day in the park."

She grinned at him, and he saw the hope reflected in her eyes. "When do you want to leave?"

"As soon as you're ready."

"Okay," she said. "I want to unpack a couple more boxes and I'll be ready. Is eleven o'clock all right?"

"Eleven o'clock it is. You've got yourself a date."

"Knock, knock."

Patsy ran her hand across her forehead. "Oh, God, not another knock-knock joke." This would make the millionth knock-knock joke he'd told today. And it was only six o'clock.

"You asked for this," Kenny said, all revved up for the joke. "Knock, knock."

"All right. Who's there?"

"You."

Patsy rolled her eyes. She knew this one was going to be bad. "You who."

"Yoo-Hoo chocolate drink," Kenny said, then fell back on the blanket, holding his stomach to control his laughter.

Kenny could do a lot of things, but telling jokes wasn't one of them. She'd have to get him another joke book. Evidently he hadn't used the one she'd given him when they were in high school. This time she'd read it to him. She looked down at him. "What are you laughing at?"

"Yoo-Hoo chocolate drink," he repeated, and kept laughing.

The joke wasn't funny, but Kenny laughed so hard it was contagious. Soon Patsy found herself laughing with him, even though she didn't get the joke. When he finally stopped laughing his eyes were full of tears.

"I still don't know why that was funny," Patsy said when her own laughter subsided.

"Then why were you laughing?"

"Because you were."

Kenny stared at her, then fell back, laughing again. "You're something else, Patsy," he said.

She lay next to him, content to laze away the rest of the afternoon staring at the sky. "You're not so bad yourself. I'm so glad we came out here today. Thank you." It had been a beautiful day. They'd gone bike riding, had flown kites, fed the ducks, rode in the paddleboats and even taken a horse ride. She couldn't have asked for a better day.

Kenny turned on his side to face her, his big smile set off by those gorgeous dimples. A woman could get lost in that smile, she thought.

"Thank you for coming with me," he said. "I haven't had this much fun since we took Wendy to the amusement park."

"That was a great day," Patsy agreed, clearly remembering that outing last summer. "Wendy was having so much fun she didn't want to go home." But this day was different. Today was a Kenny-and-Patsy day, something they hadn't really shared since they were kids.

Kenny grunted. "That's natural for her. She has limitless energy. Unlike her old man. I tire pretty fast."

"Oh, I don't know about that. You handled yourself well on the bike ride."

Kenny pulled up a blade of grass and ran it down her nose, "You're saying that because you beat me to the top of the hill."

"I've always been a gracious winner," Patsy teased.

He grimaced. "And such a modest one."

"I'll have to tell Wendy about the race. I'm sure she'll want to see a rematch."

"So now you want to embarrass me in front my daughter. That's not a motherly thing to do, Mama Patsy."

Patsy closed her eyes and ran her tongue across her lips. He wondered if she'd look that content after they'd made love.

"Say it again," she said.

"What?"

"Mama Patsy."

"Okay, Mama Patsy." The words rolled off his tongue, delighting her. "You like that name, do you?"

She opened her eyes, and her answer was plain for him to see. "I love it. You know how much I wanted kids when Theo and I were first married, Kenny. And when things started to go sour for us, I prayed I wouldn't get pregnant. That was a hard time for me. As much as I wanted a baby, I didn't want one in a bad marriage. That's not fair to the child."

"Would you still be with Theo if you'd gotten pregnant?"

"Yes," Patsy answered without hesitation. "I would have done everything in my power to make a happy home with Theo, for the sake of our child."

"Do you think it would have worked?"

She shrugged. "Who knows? Maybe. Maybe not. But I know I couldn't have left him. He would have had to leave me."

Kenny didn't respond immediately. If Theo had gotten Patsy pregnant, she wouldn't be with him now. For some reason, that thought scared him.

"Patsy?" he said a few minutes later.

"What?" she asked in a quiet voice.

"I'm glad you didn't get pregnant."

Patsy smiled from her soul. "I'm glad, too."

Kenny moved closer to her until his shoulder touched hers, then he took her hand in his. It was a comforting move, not a sexual one. As he held her hand and stared into the sky, he thanked God for giving them both a second chance.

Chapter Eleven

Patsy stepped back from the kitchen table and assessed her handiwork. She smiled. Not bad for a first-timer. She leaned her head to the side to make sure the cake was level. Thank goodness for vanilla icing, she thought. And thank God kids loved icing, since one corner of the sheet cake had more icing than cake.

Satisfied, she opened the box of pink-and-green flowers and began lining the top of the cake. That done, she picked up the fat tube of chocolate and squeezed out *Happy Birthday, Wendy.* Patsy stepped back again. Much, much better, she said to herself.

For the final touch, she opened the box of thin, green-and-pink candles and stuck seven of them in the cake, knowing they'd plant more firmly before the icing stiffened. All she needed to do now was light the candles. Unfortunately, that would have to wait until tomorrow.

For tonight, she'd wrap the cake and put it in the refrigerator.

"That looks good," Kenny said when he entered the kitchen, his hands and shirt streaked with ink from the magic markers he'd been using to make the banner.

"Good enough to eat?" she asked.

He dipped a finger in the bowl of leftover icing and licked it off with his tongue. "You betcha."

"Do you think Wendy will like it?"

"If it's sweet, Wendy'll like it. Take my word for it. Leah always...." Kenny began, but he stopped.

Patsy put a hand on his wrist. "It's all right to talk about her, Kenny. She's Wendy's mother and as much a part of this family as I am."

"She's dead, Patsy."

"That only means she's not here in person. But she's here." She placed her hand on his chest. "And in Wendy's heart. Have you been thinking about her a lot today?"

Kenny nodded solemnly. "Wendy's birthday is tough. Leah always made a big deal out of it." He smiled at his memories. "Every year she had to outdo what she'd done the previous year. When Wendy was three, she had horses brought in and all the kids had horse rides. They loved it."

"I bet you did too," Patsy added softly.

"Those were good times for us. Real good times." He wished all their times together had been that good. But it was too late for wishes. Much too late.

"You never told me about the horses. I want to see the video. I know Leah made one."

"Yeah, Leah made a tape," Kenny said. He thought about the late nights during her illness when Leah, unable to sleep because of her pain, had asked him to play the tapes for her. Unfortunately, as the end drew nearer, those nights became more and more frequent. But it seemed the tapes gave her comfort. She'd watch them over and over, as if she was recording in her mind everything about her life with him and Wendy.

"Do you think I could watch it one night?" she asked, interrupting his thoughts.

Kenny shrugged. "Sure. If you want to."

She smiled. "I want to. Do you want to watch with me?"

"I don't know, Patsy. I haven't watched those movies since Leah died."

Patsy turned her attention back to the cake. "I understand, Kenny," she said, and she did. She understood that Kenny still had a lot of grieving to do for Leah and that he wasn't ready to do it yet. She knew it also meant that he wasn't ready yet to move forward with his life, even though he said he was. Thank goodness their friendship was solid enough that she could give him the time and space he needed to get ready.

Kenny reached around her and stuck his finger in the bowl of leftover icing again. "This is so good it made me forget why I came in here. I want you to come look at my decorations."

Patsy quickly placed the cake in the refrigerator and followed Kenny into the foyer, where red, blue, yellow, orange and green balloons floated. A banner reading Happy Birthday, Wendy in the colors smeared on Kenny's hands and shirt hung about five feet from the door. Multicolored streamers were looped around the entrance.

"It looks great, Kenny."

"Not too much?"

She shook her head. "Not at all. Wendy's going to love it, and so will all the other kids."

"I want this to be a special birthday for her," he said. "It's amazing to me that she's still a happy little girl after all she's been through."

"That's because of what you and Leah gave her, and what you continue to give her, Kenny. Wendy's happy because she's loved and always has been."

"I still remember the day Leah told me she was pregnant. It had to be the happiest day of my life." His lips turned up in a sheepish grin. "Every time I said that, Leah would correct me and say it was a tie for the happiest day."

"What was the other day?"

Kenny cleared his throat, and Patsy knew he wished he hadn't started this line of conversation. "Our wedding day."

"Leah was a special woman, Kenny. She gave you and Wendy something to hang on to after she was gone. She gave you each other, and she gave you confidence in the love she had for both of you."

Kenny opened his mouth to say he wasn't so sure about that, but instead he said, "She was a special woman." She had been, but that wasn't what he was thinking. He was wondering how Leah had really felt about him before she died. Had she still loved him or had his misplaced priorities killed her love? She'd told him over and over that she loved him. And sometimes he believed her. Believed that maybe she'd seen the change in him and seen that he cared more for his family than he did for his work.

"I think Leah is proud of what you've done since she's been gone, Kenny."

"You think so?" he asked, and realized Patsy's answer was important to him.

She tilted her head back a little. "You know what I

remember most about Leah? I remember the nights
Wendy would lie in bed with her and sing to her. It must
have been difficult for Leah to have Wendy see her the
way she was. But she was strong. She thought more of
Wendy than she did of herself. And I think that's why
Wendy's so happy now. Leah didn't allow her to be
afraid. She wouldn't want you to be afraid, either,
Kenny. Not of anything. Leah promised Wendy a new
mommy. That meant she promised you a new wife.
Grieve for her, Kenny. It's time.''

Patsy's eyes were full of tears and her heart was heavy
when she finished speaking, so she didn't know if she
opened her arms to Kenny for comfort or to be comforted. All she knew was that she needed to hold him
and he needed to be held.

A happy, sleepy Wendy and her tired and happy
grandparents arrived later that night. Kenny and Patsy
got some idea of how sleepy the little girl was when her
only response to the decorations was, ''Balloons. Daddy
got me balloons.''

''Daddy sure did,'' Patsy had said, following Kenny
up the stairs to put the little darling to bed.

Wendy fell asleep so quickly that Patsy and Kenny
had to undress her and put on her pajamas. As they stood
near her bed and watched her sleep, Patsy felt like a real
parent. She couldn't imagine caring for a child from her
own body any more than she cared for the precious child
lying there.

She sat on the edge of the bed and rubbed her hand
softly across Wendy's forehead. ''The poor darling is
exhausted.''

''All this sleep means she'll be at warp speed tomorrow. A part of me is tempted to wake her up for that very reason.''

Patsy looked up at Kenny, seeing right through him. ''If you woke her up, which you're not going to do, it would be because you've missed her so much you can't wait to talk to her.''

''You're right. The little bugger needs to wake up and talk to her daddy.''

Patsy kissed Wendy's forehead, then got up from the bed. ''Let her sleep, Kenny.''

He leaned down and kissed Wendy as she had done. ''Sleep tight, Peanut. And don't let the bedbugs bite.''

When Kenny and Patsy got back downstairs, Leah's parents were getting ready to go to a hotel.

''You don't have to do that,'' Patsy said to the older couple. ''Kenny and I have your room all ready for you.''

''Not this time, dear,'' Mrs. Ellis said. ''You and Kenny don't need two old people underfoot.''

''Don't even think that, Mrs. Ellis,'' Patsy said. ''You're always welcome here. Always.''

Mrs. Ellis patted Patsy's hand. ''I know, dear,'' she said. ''But we'd prefer the hotel. We have guaranteed reservations, so we'd have to pay, anyway.''

''We'll be back in the morning for breakfast—'' Mr. Ellis began, but his wife cut him off.

''George, you can't go around inviting yourself to breakfast.''

''Nonsense, Juanita. Kenny fixes the best breakfast I've ever eaten.''

''Of course you'll come here for breakfast,'' Kenny said. ''And that's not open to negotiation, Mother Ellis.''

''If you're sure it's all right?'' Leah's mother said, looking at Patsy.

Patsy took the older woman's hand in hers. "You're always, always welcome here, Mrs. Ellis. You're Wendy's grandmother. My marriage to Kenny doesn't change that."

"And it doesn't change the way I feel about either of you," Kenny added. "I hope you know that."

Mr. Ellis clapped Kenny on the back. "We understand, son. But you know women. Sometimes they get all confused."

Mrs. Ellis rolled her eyes and Patsy smiled.

"Leah always liked you, Patsy," Mrs. Ellis whispered when the men had moved toward the door. "She sang your praises often. I know it gives her peace to know you're taking care of Wendy and Kenny."

Patsy embraced the other woman. "Thank you so much for saying that. I hope we can get to know each other better and become friends."

"After all you did for my daughter when she was ill, I already consider you one. You were a true friend to her, Patsy, and I won't forget that. If you ever need my help with anything, and I mean anything, you let me know."

Patsy nodded, glad to have the older woman's approval and support.

"Well, dear," Mrs. Ellis said in a voice loud enough for the men to hear. "We'd better get to the hotel and rest our tired old bones."

"Speak for yourself, woman," Mr. Ellis called. "My bones may be old, but they're not tired."

"And they say we're vain," the older woman chided softly.

Kenny and Patsy stood on the front step and waved to the older couple until they were out of the driveway.

When they stepped back inside, Kenny asked, "So what do we do now?"

"Well," Patsy offered. "We could finish decorating the family room and the deck."

"Yeah, we could do that."

"Or we could wrap the few gifts that we haven't wrapped already."

"Yeah, we could do that, too."

"Or," she said with a broad smile, "we could go upstairs and watch Wendy sleep some more."

Kenny grinned, and she knew he'd been thinking the same thing. "I'll race you," he said, and took off for the stairs with Patsy close behind him.

The next night Patsy and Kenny were the tired and sleepy ones. After all the guests had gone home and they'd put a reluctant, but still deliriously happy Wendy to bed, they went downstairs to make a final assessment of the damage and make a dent toward clearing the party zone so it looked like a home again.

"We're not getting much done sitting here with our feet propped up on the coffee table," Kenny said. He pushed a piece of crepe paper with his foot. "The cluttered coffee table."

"You're right," Patsy said, hating to even think about the work that needed to be done in the kitchen. "You'd think we had a hundred kids here today instead of twenty. I don't remember Wendy's parties getting out of hand like this before."

"Neither do I. It must have been all that icing on your cake. It really hyped the little devils up."

Patsy grinned, relieved her cake had been such a hit with the kids. "They did like it, didn't they?"

Kenny grunted. "That's an understatement. I thought

Audrey Simmons and Mary Jones were going to fight over that last piece. I've never seen anything like it.''

"Neither had their mothers," Patsy said with a laugh. "You should have see the looks on their faces. It was priceless.''

"I didn't have time to do anything as tame as watching the parents. I was too busy trying to keep that Adams boy from slugging the Willis girl in the face. I'm glad her mother didn't see that.''

"I didn't, either.''

"Take my word for it, it was ugly. Very ugly.''

Patsy laughed. The kids had been a handful, but it had all been worth it to see the look of pure joy on Wendy's face. "I think that means it was a great party.''

"Wendy'll probably be talking about it until next year.''

"I certainly hope so. I wanted it to be special for her. I'm just sorry Marilyn couldn't make it.'' Patsy's friend had dropped her gift by minutes before the party started and had told Patsy she was on her way to visit her sick mother.

"I hope her mother gets better," Kenny said.

"Me, too.''

"Well, it should make you happy to know that Derrick asked about her.''

"He did?'' Patsy's eyes lit up, and Kenny thought he saw himself in them. "What did he say?''

"He wanted to know where she was. When I told him she'd gone to visit her mother, he looked relieved.''

"I wonder what that was all about," Patsy said.

"Well, I don't. Let's not talk about Marilyn and Derrick tonight.'' Kenny slid his long legs to the floor and turned to Patsy. He pulled a string of ribbon, probably from one of Wendy's gifts, out of her hair and handed it to her. "A memento for you."

She held it to her heart, Derrick and Marilyn quickly forgotten. "I'll cherish it forever," she said in a mock Scarlett O'Hara voice.

"There's plenty more where that came from. I can get some for you if you want it."

Patsy shook her head. "This is enough."

"You're serious about keeping that ribbon, aren't you?"

"Yes, I'm serious. I want to remember this day always." She peeked over at Kenny. "I kept a couple of the invitations, too."

"You're incredible," he said.

"Why, thank you, sir. I'm glad you noticed."

"Oh, I've noticed, all right. I've noticed a lot."

A warm feeling spread through Patsy's body. "Like what?"

"Fishing for compliments?"

"A girl has to do what a girl has to do."

Kenny shook his head. "You're almost as bad as Wendy."

"Does that mean you aren't going to compliment me, Daddy?"

Kenny laughed at Patsy's imitation of Wendy in one of her finer moments. "You're worse than Wendy."

"But Daddy..." Patsy continued.

Kenny held up his hands. "Stop it already. I'll give you a compliment. Or two."

Patsy primly clasped her hands and placed them across her stomach. "You were saying?" she prompted.

"I thought I knew everything there was to know about you," he began, "but I learn something new everyday. I knew you wanted kids, but I never knew how much making Wendy your daughter would mean to you. I knew you loved her, but I had no idea how much. You love her as much as I do, and I didn't think that was possible."

Patsy kept her eyes closed and didn't speak.

"Hey, you aren't crying under there, are you?"

Patsy shook her head, but he was sure she was crying.

"That's another thing. I knew you were an old softy, but I didn't realize how quickly joy or sadness made you cry. I don't think you've cried as much in all the years I've known you as you've done in the last few weeks. What I don't know is if that's good or bad."

She still didn't say anything. He pulled on the sleeve of her plaid shirt. "Is it good or bad?"

"It's good," she said in a voice choked with tears.

"Do you want me to stop?" he asked softly.

She shook her head.

"Did you know that you were beautiful?"

Her brows lifted at that question, but her eyes remained closed.

"You are. And you get more beautiful every day. It doesn't matter what you wear. You're as beautiful tonight, tired and in your worn jeans, as you were on our wedding day. Ahh, I'll never forget how you looked that day, Patsy. You were an angel. My own, dark, beautiful angel."

"Kenny," she said, her voice pleading.

"And you're still my dark, beautiful angel tonight." He traced a finger down her jaw. "Your skin is so soft. Has it always been that way? It seems that I would've noticed that a long time ago. It's not like I haven't touched you before."

"Kenny..." she pleaded again.

He moved his hands up to her hair. "I wonder about

this sometimes. I wonder how you'll look after a night of making love to me. Will your hair stay in place or will it be all over your head?''

''Kenny...'' Her voice was weaker.

''I hope it'll be all over your head. I want you out of control. But you know what I like best?''

''Don't...'' she warned.

''It's not your breasts, though they're great. Full, the way I like them. When I hold them in my hands, I know they'll spill over.''

Patsy squeezed her eyes tighter.

''And it's not your legs, though God knows you have a great set of legs. I had to stop looking at them because I couldn't keep my mind from wondering how it would feel to have them wrapped around me.''

''Enough!''

''No. I like your eyes best. You know why? Because they're open and honest. Whenever I want to know the truth, all I have to do is look in your eyes. They tell me everything I want to know. And, I assure you, there are some things I could do without knowing.''

He pulled on her sleeve again. ''Will you open your eyes for me, baby? I want to know what you're thinking.''

''No, Kenny...''

''Yes, baby,'' he coaxed. ''I want to look in those deep brown eyes and see whether you're growing to care as much for me as I'm growing to care for you. Please.''

He watched as she slowly opened her eyes. Though they were filled with tears, he saw what he wanted to see. Hearing her say the words would make it perfect, but he wouldn't ask her to voice what he saw in her eyes tonight. No, he'd wait for that.

''Patsy, will you do something for me?''

She blinked a couple of times before answering him. "What?"

"Will you kiss me?"

"We shouldn't," she said.

"I know that, but I want to. Just one kiss." He raised his hand in the Boy Scout pledge. "I promise it won't go any further than one kiss."

He watched as her eyes closed again and her head turned ever so slightly in his direction. That was all the encouragement he needed. He reached for her and she came willingly into his arms. When his lips met hers, he found welcome. And hunger. His for her. And hers for him.

She moaned and pushed closer against him when his tongue slipped past her lips. He responded by crushing her to him. He wondered for a short second if he was holding her too tightly. But when she wrapped her arms around his shoulders, all thought of everything but their kiss left his mind.

Control came to him from a place he didn't know he had, and he soon lifted his mouth from hers, taking one final nip at her lips before letting her go. Her eyes were still closed, and though he wanted more than anything to see his passion for her mirrored in them, he respected her privacy.

He rubbed his forefinger along her now-swollen lips, then murmured, "Thank you."

Patsy didn't say anything, and he didn't, either. He lay back on the couch next to her and thought that life could only get better with her by his side.

Chapter Twelve

"Wendy," Patsy said, getting up from the table and taking her dishes with her. Kenny had prepared breakfast, so her job was clearing the table. "It's time for school. Go wash up so we can leave."

Wendy quickly gulped the last of her milk. "Okay, Mama Patsy," she said, scrambling down from the table.

"Slow down, Wendy," Kenny called her as she raced away. He shook his head, then turned back to Patsy. "She's getting worse every day."

Patsy cleared the rest of the dishes from the table and stacked them in the dishwasher. "You love it and you know it. She's happy, Kenny. Really happy."

Patsy felt Kenny walk up behind her, so she wasn't surprised when his hands enclosed her waist. After the kiss they'd shared the night of Wendy's party two weeks ago, she'd been afraid they'd crossed a line they wouldn't be able to come back from. She'd even lain awake in bed that night, praying Kenny wouldn't knock on her door. But there'd been no need. He hadn't come that night or any of the nights after.

The kiss hadn't been the turning point she'd dreaded; instead, it had cleared the air between them. They both understood the depth of their attraction for each other and knew that the time wasn't right for anything more. So they'd settled into a comfortable, nonthreatening and, she admitted, sometimes frustrating relationship. But she was happy. And he was happy. And most importantly, Wendy was happy.

Patsy turned in Kenny's arms and smiled up at him. "What?" she asked.

"Thank you," he said.

"For what?"

He kissed her on the tip of her nose, then dropped his arms from her waist and stepped back. "For being you."

"No need to thank me for that. It's pretty easy to be myself."

"Mama Patsy," Wendy called from the foyer. "I'm ready."

"Okay, sweetheart. We're coming." Patsy closed the dishwasher and followed Kenny out to the foyer.

"Do you have your books?" she asked Wendy. The youngster held up her books. "And your homework?"

Wendy pulled out two sheets of ruled tablet paper and smiled up at her. "You ask me that every morning."

Patsy brushed down an unruly strand of hair that had come loose from one of the little girl's braids. "That's because I don't want you to forget anything."

Kenny handed Patsy her briefcase. "And I don't want you to forget anything."

Their routine comforted Patsy. Her morning ride with Wendy was the highlight of her day. She and Kenny had decided that she would drive Wendy to school in the mornings on her way to her office and he'd pick her up after school. That way each of them had some private time with her each day. Patsy thought Wendy liked the new routine as much as they did.

"My girls all ready?" Kenny asked, opening the door for them.

"All ready," Wendy said. She hugged her father, then took the lunch box he handed to her. "See you after school, Daddy."

Kenny tugged on one of her braids. "I'll be there, Peanut. Have fun."

Wendy skipped out the door and to the car.

Kenny kissed Patsy on the cheek. "You have a good day, too. I'll see you tonight."

"That's a deal, buster," she said, and rushed to the car.

Her morning drive was filled with Wendy's cheerful chatter, as usual. And Patsy savored every minute of it.

When they reached the school, Wendy leaned over and gave her a short hug before jumping out of the car and running to meet her friends. Patsy smiled all the way to her office.

Right after lunch, Kenny phoned her.

"Look, Patsy," he said anxiously. "I just got a call from the school. Wendy's crying and won't stop. Mrs. Walden thinks we need to get over there."

Patsy clutched her hand to heart. Oh, God, she prayed, please don't let anything be wrong with my little girl. "What is it, Kenny?"

"She's not physically hurt or anything. Mrs. Walden says they can't get her to stop crying. She'll pause and try to tell Mrs. Walden what's wrong, and then she'll start crying all over again."

His words eased Patsy's anxiety some, but her heartbeat still raced. "I'll meet you at the school."

"No," Kenny said firmly. "Come home and we'll drive over together."

"But the time, Kenny..." she began, wanting to be with Wendy, not wasting her time driving home.

"Calm down, Patsy. It'll only be five minutes more. Come here and we'll drive to the school together."

"Okay, okay," she said. She needed to get a grip on herself. It wouldn't do for Wendy to see her like this. Her anxiety would only cause the child to become more anxious herself.

Patsy saw Kenny standing in the driveway as soon as she turned onto their street. When she pulled up, he rushed around to the driver's side and opened her door.

"Slide over," he said. "I'll drive."

She did as he asked without question. "Do you really think she's all right?"

Kenny clasped her hand in his own in an attempt to calm her, she knew. "She's not all right, but she's not hurt, either. We'll find out what's wrong and she'll be fine."

Patsy squeezed Kenny's fingers and prayed he was right. Wendy's cheerful face appeared in her mind. "What could have happened, Kenny? She was perfectly fine when I dropped her off this morning."

"I know," he said. "But we'll find out in a couple of minutes. We're almost at the school."

The short drive to the school seemed to take an exceptionally long time to Patsy. When they finally arrived, Kenny had to grab her arm to keep her from jumping out of the car and running inside.

"We have to be calm," he said, telling her what she

already knew. "If we're going to help Wendy, we have to be calm. Now take a deep breath."

Patsy took a deep breath and it helped. A little. "I'm ready," she said.

Kenny studied her for a few long seconds, then leaned across her and opened her door. When they reached the school, a secretary directed them to the room where Mrs. Walden sat with Wendy.

Patsy's heart crumbled when she saw her little girl curled in Mrs. Walden's arms, her sniffles so loud Patsy wondered why the whole school didn't hear them. At least, they sounded that loud to her.

Patsy rushed to Mrs. Walden and knelt down next to her. She gently rubbed Wendy's back. "What's the matter, sweetheart?"

Wendy raised her head, then launched herself into Patsy's arms. "Oh, Mama Patsy," she said between sniffles. "I'm so glad you're here. Where's Daddy?"

Kenny crouched down next to them. "I'm right here, Peanut," he said, using his fingers to wipe away her tears. "What's wrong with my big girl?"

"Oh, Daddy," the child cried, reaching to include him in her embrace.

The three of them stayed like that until Wendy's sniffles stopped. Kenny wiped at her tears again, then asked, "What happened, honey? What made Daddy's girl cry?"

Wendy lifted her tear-streaked eyes to Mrs. Walden.

"Go ahead and tell them, darling," the older woman coaxed. "They want to know."

Patsy shot a glance at Mrs. Walden, and again she was struck with a definite sense of familiarity. She would have sworn she knew the woman from someplace.

"M-Meg Thomas said you were get—getting a divorce," Wendy said in a choked voice.

Patsy raised shocked eyes to Kenny.

"That's not true, Wendy." Kenny rubbed her back as he spoke to her with infinite patience. Patsy, on the other hand, wanted to spank that Meg Thomas but good. "Patsy and I just got married," he continued. "We're not getting a divorce."

Kenny looked up at Mrs. Walden. "Meg Thomas should be punished for saying that to Wendy. It was cruel."

"But—but you don't s-sleep in the—the same room," Wendy said, and her sniffles started again.

Patsy and Kenny shot each other another glance.

"Meg says that—that means you're g-getting a di-divorce."

"Oh, Wendy," Patsy said, hating the pain the other girl's words had caused her daughter, while realizing she and Kenny were the ultimate source of her pain.

"She said her first mommy and daddy lived in separate rooms and then they got divorced."

The little girl's eyes told them she wanted an explanation for their sleeping arrangements, an explanation she could understand.

"What Audrey said about us is not true, Wendy," Kenny began. "Your Mama Patsy and I are not getting a divorce." Patsy noted he didn't give a reason for their separate rooms.

"Then why don't you sleep in the same room?" the incorrigible tyke asked, her voice now clear.

"Well," Kenny began. "Your Mama Patsy and I have always had our own rooms."

From the bewildered look on Wendy's face, Patsy knew the child wasn't buying her father's line.

"All the other kids say their mommy and daddy sleep in the same room. Why do you have to sleep in different rooms?"

Patsy sneaked a quick glance at Mrs. Walden, who had found a sudden interest in her fingernails.

"It's only temporary, Wendy," Patsy said, glad she didn't have to lie. "Until I'm used to my new home." Patsy thought she saw understanding light Wendy's eyes.

"Aren't you used to it already?"

Apparently, Patsy had read the child wrong. She turned to Kenny, who, to her dismay, was grinning. "What are you smiling at?" she asked.

Kenny shrugged. "I'm waiting to hear your answer to Wendy's question. Aren't you used to it already?"

As Patsy, Kenny and Wendy moved her belongings into Kenny's room later that night, Patsy couldn't rid herself of the feeling she'd been suckered by a seven-year-old. But that was impossible, wasn't it?

She glanced at Kenny and Wendy as they moved his shoes to the rear of the closet to make room for hers. Surely Kenny hadn't planned this with Wendy, had he?

She shook her head to clear the cobwebs she knew had to be wrapped around her brain. "He couldn't be that devious."

"Something wrong, Patsy?" Kenny called from across the room.

"No, no," she said. She hadn't realized she'd spoken aloud. "Everything's fine." Just perfect, she repeated in her mind. Just darn perfect.

Kenny leaned back against the headboard of his king-size bed, a sour smirk on his face instead of the great big grin his good luck should have placed there. He'd gotten what he wanted. Or what he thought he'd wanted. He'd gotten Patsy in his bed. Too bad she was about as excited about it as a convict facing the gallows.

The look of horror on her face when Wendy had asked if she was used to her new home yet and her subsequent attempt to explain their relationship to his daughter had made him grin. Now, though, he couldn't find the humor in their situation.

He turned to the bathroom door, then glanced at the clock sitting on the headboard. Patsy had been in there an hour, if not longer. What was she doing? he wondered. He wouldn't be surprised if she came out dressed in a suit of armor. As a matter of fact, a part of him wished she would. It would make this night much, much easier to endure.

He heard the bathroom door squeak and immediately slid down in the bed and pulled the covers over himself, but not before quickly checking to make sure that every button on his rarely worn cotton pajamas was fastened. He didn't want any of his private body parts embarrassing either of them.

He squinted an eye and saw Patsy tiptoe to the bed, trying not to wake him. She didn't have on a suit of armor, but what she wore came close. If the top button on that white flannel gown was any closer to her neck, he was sure she'd strangle herself. Then there were the sleeves, so long she had to roll them up to see her hands. He smiled when he took in the fluffy house shoes with the mouse ears. She probably wore those every night, but he would bet all his money she'd never worn that gown before.

He couldn't talk too much about her, though. He couldn't remember the last time he'd worn a pajama top *and* bottoms. He usually wore only the latter, and he did that mostly for Wendy's sake. When she wasn't home, he preferred to sleep nude.

When Patsy slid her slim body under the covers, he turned over, still pretending he was asleep. Through squinted eyes, he could see that she had her ramrod-straight back to him. She was so close to the edge of the bed that if he touched her leg she'd fall on the floor.

He turned again to lie flat on his back and stared at the ceiling. What the hell? he thought. "Patsy?"

He felt her tense up. "Yes?" she replied softly.

"I'm really sorry about this. I wouldn't have made an issue of it until you were ready."

"I know."

"Are you all right?"

"Yes, I'm fine."

She didn't sound fine. "Are you sleepy?"

She sighed. "Not really."

He turned so he faced her back and leaned his head on his hand. "Then why don't you turn on the light so we can talk?"

She reached up and switched on the light on her nightstand, then turned around to face him. The glow from the lamp illuminated the soft, clear features of her face, and he thought again that she looked like an angel.

"What do you want to talk about?" she asked.

"This," he said, extending his hand across the bed. "How you feel about being in this bed with me."

"How do you feel about it?"

"Frustrated," he answered truthfully.

Her soft laugh caused his insides to go all mushy. "I know the feeling."

"Well, at least we're even."

"I guess that's something."

"You don't have to be afraid of me, you know," he said.

"I'm not afraid of you."

She was afraid of *something*. "Then why are you so close to the edge of the bed? There's plenty of room. We could drive a tractor trailer through the space between us."

"I know you're used to having the whole bed to yourself. If you're anything like me, you probably sleep all over the bed. I didn't want to get in your way."

What she didn't want was for him to touch her, he knew. Well, he didn't want that, either. Not yet. Not until he could touch her the way he wanted to. "Why don't we divide the bed in half? The juncture where our pillows meet can be the dividing line."

"But you need more space, don't you? You're bigger."

He shook his head. "This is a king-size bed. I'm not that big."

She looked as if she wasn't too sure about that, but she nodded anyway.

"Hey, Patsy, this is as hard for me as it is for you. The best thing for us to do is keep it simple. You need to relax, loosen up. If we don't make it a big deal, it won't be a big deal. We've slept in the same bed before, anyway."

"We were kids then, Kenny, not husband and wife. There's a difference."

He shook his head in disagreement. "Not if we don't let there be." He waited for his words to sink in. "Now tell me about your morning before my phone call."

She started out hesitantly, but gradually she relaxed, and they talked as if they were sitting across from each other sharing a cup of coffee.

When she yawned, he said, "I guess that means it's time for the light to go out."

"You're right. It's my turn to cook breakfast in the morning, so I have to get up first."

Kenny slid down in the bed. "That's right. And be sure to be quiet when you get up. I need my beauty sleep."

"Hah," she said, then kicked him in the leg. "I hate to tell you this, but you've waited too late. The face you have is the face you're stuck with. I don't care how long you sleep."

He laughed and contentment settled in his bones. He and Patsy were going to make it. If they could handle sleeping together without really sleeping together when they both wanted to sleep together, they could handle anything. "Good night, Patsy," he said.

She reached up and turned out the light. "Night, Kenny."

He grinned in the darkness.

A few minutes later, she added, "Don't let the bedbugs bite."

Their combined laughter was the last thing he heard before he drifted off to sleep.

Chapter Thirteen

Patsy knew she was in trouble when she opened her eyes and saw the expanse of bed in front of her, felt the strong, warm bands around her waist and felt Kenny's hard body pressed against the length of hers. Evidently, she'd rolled toward his warmth during the night. And apparently, he hadn't pushed her away. What was she going to do now?

She touched the warm arm around her waist and marveled that such a strong, hard man could be so tender with Wendy. And with her. Feeling bold, she traced her slim fingers over his ring finger, starting at the nail and traveling down to the base, which was covered with the simple gold wedding band she'd given him. An involuntary shiver wracked her body and she sucked in her breath, praying Kenny wouldn't wake up.

When he didn't awaken, she relaxed, but she didn't resume her exploration of his body. She knew her weakness for him could turn a pleasurable examination into a passionate encounter that she wasn't ready to deal with. She grew more ready every day, felt more confident of Kenny's growing feelings for her, but she was still pretty sure he hadn't finished grieving for Leah. She knew it was senseless to wait for him to get over Leah before giving herself fully to him, but she did want his grief to be behind him. And she was prepared to wait until it was.

Patsy closed her eyes, stopped analyzing her situation and allowed herself to enjoy the uncomplicated closeness she shared with Kenny. She felt protected in his arms as she always did in his presence, but she also felt contentment, a feeling she hadn't named before. There was something right about being in bed with him like this. Holding each other. She knew it wouldn't be long before they could enjoy their closeness without reservation.

She drifted back into a peaceful sleep, telling herself there was plenty of time left before she had to get up.

Even after he knew she'd fallen asleep, Kenny didn't move. Every part of his body was hard and begging. And if he moved now, one part of his anatomy would press against her. Flannel gown or no flannel gown, she'd feel him, and that would surely wake her up. And she'd be embarrassed. He'd be embarrassed, too, and he didn't want that. He didn't want her to find out that he'd known the very moment her soft, alluring woman's body had rolled next to his throbbing male one.

But he had. He closed his eyes and savored the memory. At first he'd thought it was a dream, and he hadn't wanted to open his eyes for fear of ending it. But he'd opened them anyway and found it wasn't a dream. Patsy was real and alive and as comfortable in his arms as if they always slept spoon-fashion.

He closed his eyes, content for now to hold her close. When he felt himself begin to drift off, he deliberately loosened his hold on her so that when she awakened the next time, she'd be able to get up without concern for waking him.

Kenny dribbled left, leaned in, then faked right. When Derrick moved right, he charged to the goal for a layup, an easy two points.

Derrick, panting hard, leaned over and rested his hands on his knees. "What's wrong with you, man? You're a demon today."

Kenny didn't bother to answer. He stepped outside the boundary behind the goal and tossed the ball in. He hadn't come here to talk. He'd come to release some of the energy that had been building up in him since he and Patsy started sharing the same bed four nights ago.

He ran forward, determined to keep Derrick from getting a shot. All Kenny had to do was pretend Derrick was Patsy. No way was she going to drive him crazy and no way was Derrick getting to the goal. The ten-to-two score in this lunchtime game of one-on-one indicated his approach was working.

Kenny's eyes studied Derrick's right hand, then his left as the ball moved back and forth. When he caught Derrick's rhythm, he moved in and stole the ball.

"Damn," he heard Derrick say as Kenny charged toward his own basket.

Swoosh! Another goal.

"No more," Derrick called when Kenny stepped out of bounds and tossed the ball to him. He caught the ball and dropped down on the court, the ball between his legs. "What's wrong with you, man? This is only a game."

Kenny didn't want to talk. He wanted to play. He still had enough pent-up energy to light New York City on Christmas Eve. No way could he go to court strung this tightly. "Come on, man. Stop being such a poor loser."

Derrick shook his head. "No way. If I'm going to die of exhaustion, it won't be from a game of basketball."

Kenny rested his hands on his hips and stalked over to Derrick. "Is sex all you think about?"

"Who said I was talking about sex?"

Kenny didn't bother to answer. He reached for the ball, but Derrick removed it from his grasp. "Patsy giving you trouble?" he inquired with a grin.

Kenny cursed. Was it that damn obvious?

"It's all your fault," Derrick continued. "You shouldn't have given her the option of not sleeping with you. Look at you. As mean as a grizzly bear. And just because you aren't getting any loving from your dear, sweet wife." He laughed.

Kenny wanted to grab Derrick's neck in both his hands and squeeze. Instead, he dropped his hands from his hips and joined his friend on the floor.

Derrick looked over at him. "I guessed right, huh?"

"Not even close," Kenny retorted.

"You can't tell me Patsy's not the reason you're playing like a madman."

Kenny gave a heavy sigh. "We're sleeping together."

"All right!" Derrick said, slapping his friend on the back. "It's about time."

Kenny shared that sentiment. It was definitely about time. Too bad Patsy didn't see it that way.

"What's wrong with you then? You weren't playing ball out there, you were waging war."

"Patsy and I are sharing the same bed, but that's about it."

"Sharing the same bed and nothing else?" Derrick repeated.

"That's what I said." Kenny told Derrick about Wendy's incident at school and its outcome.

Derrick shook his head. "I don't believe it. I really don't believe it. It's unnatural to sleep with a woman, especially your wife, and not make love to her. Don't you know anything at all about women?"

Kenny shot his friend a bold glare. "I know enough to find a woman to share my life."

"But not enough to get her to make love with you," Derrick finished for him. "Do you want me to give you some pointers?" he asked with a straight face.

Kenny moved to get up. "Forget it, man. You're no help."

Derrick grabbed his friend's arm to keep him in place. "Come on, man. I'm only kidding."

"This isn't a kidding matter, Derrick. I'm dying."

"It can't be that bad."

"Oh, but it is." Kenny still felt the softness of Patsy's warm body as it had pressed against him this morning. Four days! This morning made four days that Patsy had rolled into his embrace during the night. God, how he wanted her. He knew he'd burst into flames if he didn't have her soon. "Patsy can't seem to stay on her side of the bed," he told Derrick. "And she's driving me crazy."

Derrick laughed, but another killing stare from Kenny cut his laughter short. "Why don't you just tell her how you feel?"

If only it were that simple, Kenny thought. "I can't.

I promised her I'd give her time. I told her I wouldn't push her. I want to keep my word.''

"The way I see it," Derrick began, "you can continue to suffer in silence or you can be honest with Patsy. Tell her how you feel. She might be as frustrated as you are. There has to be some reason she can't stay on her side of the bed.''

Kenny considered his friend's words. He knew Patsy enjoyed being in his arms; that wasn't the question. No, the question was whether her mind was ready to agree with her body. Did she trust him enough to make their marriage a real one?

Kenny looked at his watch, then stood up. "Gotta go, man. I have to be in court at one-thirty.''

"Tell her how you're feeling, Kenny," Derrick called after him.

Kenny seriously considered his friend's suggestion.

When Patsy climbed into bed four nights later in a pink version of her trademark flannel gown, he wondered how many colors the dratted garment came in. He'd seen shades of blue, white, green, red, yellow and now pink in the eight days they'd been sleeping together. He guessed she'd have to start repeating colors pretty soon.

Her scent wafted over to him, not allowing him to pull his eyes away from her. She'd washed her hair tonight. The fresh sheen told him so. She never wore rollers to bed, for which he was grateful. Her becoming hairstyle was maintenance free and she didn't even curl it in the morning, just brushed it into place. Obviously, the only moving she did during the night was to roll into his arms, because when he woke up, her hair was still in place—a fact that annoyed and tantalized him. He dreamed of planting his hands in that hair and destroying some of its tidiness.

"Did you and Derrick play ball again today?" she asked, once she was settled on her side of the bed.

He wondered why she didn't just roll into his arms now, since that's where she'd be before the night was over. He knew it and she knew it. So why were they playing this game?

"Yeah," he answered. "We played today."

"It's getting to be a habit, isn't it? Maybe I should start working out so I can keep in shape."

Kenny didn't think she needed any exercise. She was firm where she needed to be firm and soft where she needed to be soft. "You're in good-enough shape."

"I don't know," she said. "Things start going south when you get close to thirty-five. I'd better get active now."

His eyes automatically went to her breasts. Thank God she wore a light bra to bed each night. Though he was sure she didn't need to, he knew if she didn't he'd be dead by now. He throbbed just thinking about waking up with his hand covering the hard pebble at the tip of her breast. He groaned.

"Are you all right?" she asked with concern. "Maybe you and Derrick are overdoing it. You shouldn't push yourself too hard, Kenny."

He knew she thought his groan was from his aching muscles. Well, a muscle was aching, but it wasn't the one she was thinking about. "Maybe you're right," he answered.

"I know I'm right. I can see you and Derrick out there now. You're both too macho to admit you're tired, so you probably run each other too hard." She smiled over at him. "Maybe you should play Derrick on Mondays,

Wednesdays and Fridays and me on Tuesdays and Thursdays. I could use the workout and you could use the break. How about it?''

A vision of Patsy in short shorts and a loose-fitting top filled his mind. No way could he handle her bumping against him, touching him, laughing up at him with those big brown eyes. No way.

"Kenny?'' she asked again. "How about it?''

"I don't know, Patsy. When would we play? You can't make it at lunchtime, can you?''

She shook her head, and Kenny knew she was thinking of an alternative. "We can play after work. Yeah, we can go down to the playground.''

"What about Wendy?'' he asked, grasping for some reason, any reason, to get that thought out of her mind.

"She'll come with us, of course. She'd love it, Kenny. What do you think?''

I think you're trying to kill me. "We'll see,'' he said. "We'll see.''

After nine straight days of waking up with Patsy in his arms and pretending he didn't notice, Kenny was at the end of his rope. He planned to talk to her about his dilemma as soon as she came out of the bathroom. Thank God her nightly ritual had dropped from her previous hour to about twenty minutes, though he still wondered what she was doing in there all that time.

Soon the door opened and she walked out, dressed in another one of those flannel gowns—this one in orange. Where in the hell did she get the darned things? he wondered. A harsh chuckle escaped his lips when he thought of her buying them in a lingerie shop. More like an army-surplus store.

"What's so funny?'' she asked, leaning against the

headboard, ready for the nightly discussion that had become part of their routine.

"Nothing. I just thought about something."

"Tell me," she coaxed.

"It was a new knock-knock joke I'd heard."

She raised her hand. "Don't tell me. I don't think I can take a knock-knock joke tonight."

"Rough day?"

She shook her head and smiled. "Probably a very bad knock-knock joke."

She looked so adorable it took all his self-control not to pull her into his arms and kiss her senseless. "Ha, Ha, ha," he said, not believing they'd been reduced to discussing knock-knock jokes. Talk about avoiding the tough topics. "Very funny."

"Unlike your knock-knock jokes," she deadpanned.

"Enough of knocking my knock-knock jokes."

Patsy rolled her eyes. "Okay. Then, are you going to take me up on my offer of a game of basketball?"

No. He couldn't add basketball to the torture of sleeping with her. "Why don't you ask Marilyn? Derrick and I get a good workout. He'd be without a partner if I started playing you." Actually, Derrick had threatened to stop playing with him if he didn't tone down his game.

"You don't want to play with me, do you, Kenny? Boy, I learn more about you every day. You're sexist!"

"No, I'm not."

"Yes, you are. How else can you explain your unwillingness to take me on?"

Kenny couldn't believe they were arguing over this inconsequential matter. "I said that's not it."

"Then what is it?"

He took a deep breath. "Us."

"Us?"

Okay, maybe he'd been wrong to think she knew the meaning of the word. "Us, Patsy. You and me. Our marriage."

"I know what the word means," she said with too much of an edge in her voice for him to miss.

So now they were going to discuss their respective vocabularies. He didn't think so. He covertly checked that all his buttons were fastened, then turned back the covers and sat facing her, his legs crossed Indian style. "We've been married two months now," he began. "Do you have any regrets?" He hadn't planned to ask that question, but he felt a sudden need to stall for time.

"No," Patsy said hesitantly. "Why would you ask something like that? Are you having regrets?"

"Not a one," he answered immediately, seeing the wheels turning in her head and not wanting them to churn up the wrong conclusion.

"So why are we discussing it? I was talking about a simple game of basketball."

He mentally counted to ten before replying. He wasn't going to let her get him off track. "Forget basketball for a minute, will you? We need to discuss our marriage."

"No need to get upset," she said. "If you want to talk about our marriage, we'll talk about our marriage. What do you want to say about it?"

How damned frustrated I am sleeping with you every night, holding you in my arms every morning and not being able to make love to you. "Look, Patsy," he began slowly, taking her feelings into consideration. "I think our marriage is working. It's just about everything I hoped it would be." Good, he told himself. Remain calm. State the facts. "In no time, you, Wendy and I have become a family. It's hard to believe we've only been married eight short weeks.''

"That's probably because we've known each other for so long.''

"I thought that at first, but now I'm not sure. The week that Wendy was in Florida with her grandparents was the first time we'd been alone, really alone, since before I married Leah and you married Theo. That week was different. Almost like we were rebuilding our relationship from scratch. Do you know what I mean?''

She nodded. "We started something new that week. A foundation based on our relationship with each other. Not you and me and Wendy. Not you, me, Wendy and Leah. And not you, me, Wendy, Leah and Theo. Just you and me.''

Her understanding gave him the courage he needed to continue the conversation. Maybe Patsy was as ready as he was to move to the next step. "We're not kids anymore, Patsy. And we aren't just best friends. We're husband and wife.''

"I know that, Kenny," she said with impatience.

"I know you know it, but how do you feel about it? Do you think that what we share is special?''

"Of course I do.''

Okay, Kenny, he told himself. Now's the time. He cleared his throat, then said, "Does that mean you're ready to make this a real marriage?''

Her eyes widened in surprise and his confidence slipped a little. Surely she'd known the conversation was leading to this point.

"Are you?" she asked.

"I don't think you have to ask that. I've been pretty clear about my feelings.'' Kenny knew what he said now would make her want to either move forward with their relationship or stay with the status quo. He continued slowly, wanting to make sure he stated his feelings clearly. "You're my wife in every sense that a man makes a woman his wife, except that we don't make love. You're my confidante, my friend, my counselor. You're mother to my child. Now I want us to come full circle. I want it all. I want you to become my lover."

Patsy stared at the comforter, not speaking. Finally, she looked up at him. "You're pretty sure about what you want, aren't you?"

Definitely. "I guess I am."

"What about Leah?" she asked quickly.

Kenny's head jerked. He hadn't expected that question. "What about her?" he asked, not able to keep the defensiveness out of his voice. "She was my wife, but she's dead now. You're alive. You're here. The only way she'll get into bed with us is if you let her. Are you going to bring her in here with us?"

Patsy sucked in her breath. "I don't want to, but what if she's already here?"

Kenny's heart contracted at the fear he heard in Patsy's voice. He took her hand in his and rubbed his thumb across her palm. "Trust me. She's not here."

"Are you in love with me, Kenny?"

His hold on her hand tightened, but he didn't say anything. What could he say? He hadn't thought about being in love. He wanted commitment from this marriage and he didn't need to romanticize his relationship with Patsy by saying he was in love with her. He loved her and that was enough.

"Are you in love with me?" he asked, instead of answering her question.

She removed her hand from his. "That's your answer—to ask me a question?"

He didn't know what she wanted him to say. "I thought we agreed before we got married that the love we shared was enough." She nodded and he continued, "Well, what we have now is even more than we had then. I think it's enough for us to move forward, Patsy. What do you think?"

"I don't know," she said, stinging from the pain of having her words slung back at her in what she thought was a callous manner.

"Well, what more are you waiting for before we make this a real marriage?"

I want you to tell me you're in love with me, she thought immediately. She was in love with him. She loved everything about him. Maybe she'd always been in love with him. Or maybe she'd fallen in love with him that day at the church. In any case, she wanted him to be in love with her. "I want to be sure you're not going to break my heart." She spoke the truth softly but clearly.

"What can I do to prove to you that I'd never deliberately hurt you?"

Nothing short of telling me you're in with love me. "I don't know."

He sighed an old man's sigh. "So where does that leave us?"

"Frustrated?" she suggested in an attempt to lighten the seriousness of the moment.

"But not for long," he declared. "You may not be sure what you want, but I am. I'm serving notice on you today. No more Kenny, Mr. Nice Guy. I'm going to do everything in my power to make you want me as much as I want you."

"You can't seduce me," she countered. "You said you'd wait until I'm ready."

"Oh, you'll be ready, all right," he promised with a masculine gleam in his dark eyes. "You'll be so ready I won't have to seduce you. You'll seduce me."

The challenging glint in his eyes told her he meant every word he'd said.

"I guess we'll have to see, won't we?" she replied, not one to back down from any challenge.

"I guess we will." He moved back under the covers on his side of the bed. "Good night, wife. Sweet dreams."

She slowly reached for the lamp switch, then slid down under the covers.

"Patsy?" His voice called out to her from his side of the bed.

"Yes?"

"Don't hold me responsible for what happens when you roll over to my side of the bed during the night."

She sucked in a deep breath that he no doubt heard. "You knew?"

"Of course I knew. I was asleep, not dead. And I would have had to be dead not to feel the softness of your body against mine."

"Why didn't you say something?" she asked in a breathless whisper.

"I didn't hear you mentioning it. Anyway, I knew if I said something you'd try to stay awake all night, and then Wendy and I would have to deal with your bad attitude every morning."

"So why tell me now?"

She felt him smile. "Since you've rolled over to me every night that we've slept in this bed, I don't think I have anything to worry about. You might try to stay awake, but I doubt you can."

Patsy couldn't respond. She was too appalled that he

knew she'd been in his arms each morning. He knew she'd been awake and that she'd chosen to stay in his arms rather than move away.

"Patsy?" he called again.

She took a deep breath. "What?"

"Sleep tight and don't let the bedbugs bite."

Chapter Fourteen

"Umm," Patsy murmured, pressing her hips more firmly against the warmth. She stretched like a cat and allowed her entire body to go limp in the strong arms that held her. When her head rolled back against the broad, hairy chest behind her, her eyes shot open. "Kenny?" she asked. "What are you doing?"

His lips parted, but she knew it wasn't to answer her question. He moved away from her a tad, and she found herself flat on her back, staring up into eyes that paralyzed her with passion. She closed her eyelids, wanting to break the spell he'd cast over her. But also wanting to hide the need she was sure he'd read in her eyes.

"Too late," he murmured, rolling his hard body on top of hers.

Her eyes flew open again when she felt his warmth against her legs and realized the buttons of her gown were open and the skirt was bunched up around her waist. When his knees pressed against her calves, her senses demanded that she grant him entrance.

She gasped, then closed her eyes when she felt the essence of him hard and long against her. His lips found hers and she was lost. She'd known it would be like this between them. Heat. Hot. Fire. Uncontrollable fire.

Her arms encircled his back and her legs wrapped around his hips as her need to have him overtook her. This time her tongue found its way into his mouth, her exploration thorough and unrelenting.

When he groaned in pleasure, she raised her hips against him, telling him what she wanted. He groaned again, then went still against her, his head falling to her shoulder. His sudden control made her feel adrift in an ocean of darkness and unfulfilled need.

"Damn," she heard him murmur.

That one word freed her from his spell. She gathered her wits and pushed against his body. "Get off me," she ordered.

He immediately rolled to one side, though he kept one heavy arm across her waist, effectively keeping her in the bed. With lightning speed she fastened the buttons of her gown and pushed it down her legs, all the while mortified that she'd fallen into his trap. He hadn't wasted any time making good on his threat. And to make sure that she understood who was in control, he'd been the one to stop.

"Don't say I didn't warn you," he cautioned, the male smugness in his voice clear despite the shortness of his breath.

She clamped her lips shut and bit back the curse on her tongue. After taking a deep breath, she said, "Move your arm so I can get dressed. It's my morning to cook breakfast. And I have to get Wendy up."

He moved his hand, surprising her by granting her request so easily. "I'll make breakfast," he offered.

"No need." She slid her feet to the floor. "I said I'd do my share around here, and at least of one of us needs to know how to keep *her* word."

"Patsy—" he began.

She turned away from him, cutting off his words, and padded to the bathroom the way she did every morning.

Kenny lay in the bed and stared at the bathroom door, remembering the feeling of Patsy's legs wrapped tight about his hips. It had taken superhuman strength to deny her what she wanted. What they both wanted. But his damn conscience had gotten the better of him and he couldn't take their passion to its inevitable end.

He knew she thought he'd planned this morning's assault, but he hadn't. He really hadn't. He'd been dreaming about her when she rolled into his arms, and he'd thought he was still dreaming.

Well, he admitted, he'd thought it for a couple of seconds. But he soon figured out she was real. Unfortunately, she'd been so soft, so warm and so willing that he hadn't been able to resist her. Hell, he hadn't even considered resisting.

He'd guessed they'd be good together, but he hadn't been prepared for the all-consuming intensity of his desire for her nor the fervor of her response. That fervor had told him it wasn't a dream. He couldn't have dreamed it, because he hadn't ever imagined they would ignite that quickly or feverishly. He knew that if he'd made love to her this morning, he'd have been satisfied beyond measure, but somehow he also knew he'd lose her trust and her respect. And he couldn't risk that. He couldn't risk losing her friendship, the relationship they'd built, because of his need for her.

Kenny closed his eyes and waited for his body to adjust to the truth his mind knew. When the bathroom door opened, a fully dressed Patsy, looking sexy as hell in a straight black skirt and bright yellow blazer, rushed by him without even looking in his direction.

"Wait a minute," he said, as she reached for the door. "Please."

"Why, Kenny?" she replied, the hurt in her voice clear. "You've made your point."

A sharp pain settled around his heart at the tension he'd caused between them. "I didn't mean to."

She spun around, and fire had replaced the hurt he'd seen in her eyes earlier. She put her hands on the luscious hips he'd only recently held in his hands and tapped the tip of one her black pumps against the floor. "What do you mean, you didn't mean to? You meant all of it, Kenny Sanders. You meant it and don't say you didn't." She didn't wait for his response. "You know something, Kenny? You're still a kid. A big kid who wants what he wants when he wants it. I'll never know why..." She stopped suddenly. "Oh, forget it." She turned and jerked open the door.

"Please, Patsy," Kenny said again, getting out of bed and rushing toward her.

"What's the point?" she asked, her back still to him, her voice impatient. "You'll say you understand and then you'll do the same thing over again."

Kenny touched her shoulder with his right hand. "Just give me five minutes." She still didn't turn around. "Please."

She closed the door, then turned and leaned against it. She looked at her watch. "You've got five minutes."

He backed away from her and sat on the edge of the bed. "You're wrong. I didn't plan this."

"Aw, come on, Kenny. At least be man enough to tell the truth."

"I am telling the truth," he said, studying his folded hands. "I didn't plan what happened. It just happened."

She rolled her eyes and he knew she didn't believe him. "You've only got four minutes left," she said. "I suggest you start getting to the point."

"I'm going to wait until you're ready," he declared.

"Oh, goody. Now let's see, how many times have I heard that?" She held up both hands. "Hmm, I think I need to pull off my shoes also."

"Don't be funny," he warned.

"I'm not." She sighed, then walked over and knelt down beside him, placing one of her hands on his knee. "You're treating me like I'm a virgin who's afraid of sex. I'm not. I enjoy sex as much as the next woman, but I'm determined that this marriage won't end up like my marriage to Theo. It won't, Kenny. I won't let it."

"I know you won't."

"You don't act like it. You're worse than some skirt chaser running after his secretary. I'm disappointed in you, Kenny."

That she didn't believe he hadn't planned their early morning attempt at lovemaking wounded him greatly, but her disappointment hurt even worse. Never before had mistrust or this new tension existed between them. He wanted it gone. "I didn't plan it," he repeated. "You have to believe me. I've never lied to you before, have I?"

Patsy stared up into his eyes and he sighed.

"Okay, I didn't plan it, but I wanted it to happen," he admitted. "You and I could be so good together if you'd give us a chance."

He felt the increased pressure of her hand on his knee,

then she said, "You want to know about good sex? Well, I can tell you all about it. I've had good sex. Wonderful sex, where I lost control of my mind and my body. It works fine for a while. But then it stops. I found myself making love and I felt nothing. Do you hear me, Kenny? I felt nothing. Do you know how scared that made me feel? Theo and I didn't have a chance."

Kenny wiped at the tears that fell unheeded down her cheeks, cursing Theo Baxter for being so insensitive. "I'm so sorry, Patsy. For everything. I hate to see you cry." He slid down next to her and pulled her into his arms. "That was the past," he said, rubbing her arms gently. "You don't have to think about it anymore. We're not like that and we won't end up like that."

"I do want you, Kenny. I do. But I'm afraid. So afraid," she admitted. "We don't have just ourselves to think about, we have Wendy."

He tipped her chin up. "This isn't about Wendy, Patsy. It's about Theo. Maybe even about your parents and their divorce. You've brought them into our bedroom, honey."

"How can you say that?" she asked, then struggled to get out of his arms.

"Because it's true," he said softly, his hands still rubbing her arms. "We're never going to have a real marriage until you get them out of here. If I could do it for you, I would, but I can't. If we're going to live in the present and be happy, you have to make peace with the past."

Kenny didn't expect her to respond and she didn't, but he knew she'd think about the things he'd said. And he hoped she'd come to a conclusion they'd both be able to live with. He hugged her closer, continuing to rub her arms comfortingly. They stayed that way until Wendy knocked on the door and asked about breakfast.

A week later, Kenny strolled through the foyer yet again and glanced out the side panels of the front door. He wasn't worried, he told himself. He just wanted Patsy to hurry up and get home. She'd called earlier and told him that she'd be late. And then she'd called again, said good-night to Wendy and told him not to wait up for her. He shook his head. Not wait up for her? She must be crazy. Of course he was going to wait up for her.

He'd gotten used to sleeping with her, frustrating as it was, and he didn't like the idea of going to bed without her. So he waited. He peeked out the side panels one more time before taking a seat on the bottom stair.

He thought about the comfortable week they'd shared since he'd asked her to get Theo and her parents out of their bedroom. They were still there, but it seemed their presence wasn't as powerful since he and Patsy had acknowledged it. She still wasn't ready to make love with him, but he knew that soon she'd be able to accept that what the two of them shared now was much more than what she'd shared with Theo. Making love for them would be a completion. It would give them another way to love and to comfort. It would cement the friendship and attraction they already shared.

He heard her car pull into the driveway and got up to greet her. Though he wore only his pajama bottoms, he stood in the open door while she got out of the car and walked to the house.

"I told you not to wait up," she said after giving him a hug.

He took her briefcase, then closed the door behind her.

"I wanted to wait up. Are you hungry? I saved you some dinner."

She turned and flashed him a high-wattage smile that made all the waiting worthwhile. "You're too good to me, Kenny."

He tapped the tip of her nose. "Why don't you go get out of those clothes while I put your dinner in the microwave?"

When she entered the kitchen a few minutes later, dressed in her robe and house shoes, her plate was already on the table. "What do you want to drink?" he asked.

"Tea, if we have any." She took a seat at the table.

"Did you finish your presentation tonight?" he asked after he'd gotten tea for both of them and sat down across from her.

She nodded between bites of her green-bean casserole. "I hope it's good enough."

"It'll be good enough."

"Why are you so confident?" she asked, then took a drink from her glass of tea.

"I know you. You don't do anything halfway. You've done your best, and if the company doesn't see it, it's their loss."

"Maybe I should hire you to be my publicity guru," she teased.

"You don't have to hire me. I'd work pro bono."

She tore her roll in half. "And when would you have time for your law practice?"

"With the new business I'd get for you and the resulting high fees I'd charge, I wouldn't have to practice law."

"You're full of it, Kenny Sanders," she said, and tossed half her roll at him.

He caught the roll and put it in his mouth. "How about a bite of that chicken?" he asked.

She laughed at him and gave him one of the two pieces of chicken she had on her plate. When she finished eating, she cleared the table and washed the few dishes they'd used while they continued to discuss their day.

"Ready?" Kenny asked when she turned from the sink.

She nodded, and he moved to her, draped an arm around her shoulder and escorted her to their bedroom, yearning for the night he wouldn't have to let her go once they got to the bed.

Patsy hummed all the way back to her office. She'd celebrate her winning presentation to the BellNorth Company with Kenny and Wendy tonight. She would have invited her secretary, but she'd already given her the afternoon off.

Patsy looked at her watch. There was still time to call Kenny and tell him not to prepare dinner. No, she'd take them out tonight. She slapped her hand on the steering wheel and shouted one of Wendy's favorite words: *"Yippee!"*

Her heart was still racing and her spirits flying when she got back to her office and found Marilyn sitting behind her desk. "Hey, girl," she said, "what's up?"

"I take it you got the account," her friend said.

Patsy did a feminine version of Michael Jackson's moonwalk. "You bet your miniskirt, I did." She lifted her arms in the air. "I wooed them. I wowed them. I got them to sign on the dotted line."

"Congratulations! This calls for a celebration, doesn't it?"

"It does, and I'm calling Kenny right now to tell him." Patsy dropped her briefcase on her desk and picked up the phone. "I'm taking them to dinner. And you, too. It'll be fun. I'll even splurge on your date."

Marilyn shook her head. "Who would I bring? I'm not seeing anybody."

"Well, I thought…" Patsy began, then stopped when Kenny answered the phone. "Guess what? I got the account!"

"Congratulations! I knew you'd do it."

She held the phone with both hands. Kenny had told her that. He always encouraged her. She'd thought a lot about him today, even with one of the biggest presentations of her career on her schedule. "Oh, Kenny. I feel wonderful and I want to celebrate. Don't cook. I'm taking you and Wendy out to dinner."

"Too late," he said.

"You've already cooked?" Patsy's excitement dimmed a little. She wanted to dress up, go out, celebrate.

"No, I've already made reservations for dinner. Your celebration. My treat."

Tears welled up in her eyes. "Oh, Kenny, you're too good to me."

"Keep remembering that." She knew he was referring to the conversation they'd had about taking their marriage to the next step. "When do you think you'll be home?" he asked.

"Early. I have a few things to tie up here. I should be there when you get back from picking Wendy up at school."

"Okay, we'll see you then. And congratulations again, Patsy. I'm so proud of you."

A wide smile spread across her face. "Thanks, Kenny."

"Anytime," he said, then hung up.

Patsy held the receiver in her hand after he'd hung up. Kenny *was* too good to her. He supported her work; he comforted her when she was hurt. He did all the things a husband did, except one. He didn't make love to her.

"Patsy," Marilyn called, interrupting her thoughts. "I guess that dreamy look on your face means you and Kenny are getting along well."

She nodded. "Better than I thought."

"Well, come on," her friend insisted. "Tell me the details. Have you two done the deed yet?"

Patsy shook her head, remembering the morning they'd almost made love. Her body throbbed at the memory. "Not yet."

"But soon?"

"I certainly hope so." Patsy couldn't stop the grin that spread across her face. It was time. Though they'd been married only nine weeks, she and Kenny had built a foundation for their marriage. He'd promised her that Leah wasn't in their bedroom, and Patsy believed she'd exorcised Theo. Yes, it was time. There was nothing keeping them from moving to the next stage.

"Well, I'm glad somebody is lucky in love."

Patsy opened her mouth to say it wasn't love, but she didn't. Why deny it? She did love Kenny. And she'd fallen in love with him. Even if he didn't love her the same way, he *did* love her. And he cared for her. That was enough to build a marriage on—the *real* marriage that Kenny wanted. "You should try marriage yourself," she suggested to Marilyn.

"Maybe one day," Marilyn said, and Patsy detected an undercurrent of sadness.

"You want to tell me about what's bothering you? Is it your mother? I thought she was doing much better."

Marilyn glanced at her watch, then shook her head. "Nothing's wrong. And Mom's fine." She picked up her purse. "Why don't we get together for lunch when you have some time? We haven't talked in a while."

"Why don't you come with us tonight? You don't need a date. It'll be fun."

"Not tonight," Marilyn repeated as she walked to the door. "Enjoy your time with your family tonight. Give Kenny and Wendy my love."

Patsy followed her, uncomfortable with the idea of Marilyn spending the evening alone. Patsy still felt her friend's sadness. "You're sure you won't come with us?"

Marilyn shook her head again. "Thanks, but not tonight. We'll get together when you have some free time."

"Promise?"

"Promise. Now finish your work so you can get home to your family."

Patsy stared at the door after her friend had gone, certain something was up and just as certain Marilyn wasn't going to talk about it. Patsy would mention the situation to Kenny tonight and see if he had any insight for her. She wanted to help her friend, but she didn't know how if Marilyn wouldn't talk to her.

Patsy moved back to her desk, opened her briefcase and pulled out the contract. She smiled. Today had been a great day. A new account. And a new understanding of her relationship with Kenny. It was time. Tonight, Kenny would have a surprise celebration.

Two hours later, Patsy closed her briefcase and slipped on her jacket. "Finally," she said, anxious to be home with Wendy and Kenny.

She opened the door and flipped off the light, her excitement building. She couldn't wait to see the look on Kenny's face when she gave him his surprise. The telephone rang as she stepped out the door. She debated answering it, telling herself the answering machine could get it.

But as she closed the door behind her, she heard Mrs. Walden's voice. Patsy turned and rushed back to the phone.

"Mrs. Walden," she said hurriedly, "is something wrong?"

"There's been an accident," the older woman said.

Patsy pressed her free hand to her chest. "An accident? Is Wendy all right?"

The older lady began speaking so fast Patsy could barely understand her. "Slow down, Mrs. Walden, I can't make out what you're saying. Now tell me again."

"Ohh," Mrs. Walden said, "it's all my fault."

Patsy slid down in her chair and forced herself to take a deep breath. "Just tell me what happened."

"Wendy fell at the playground," the older lady finally was able to say. "And it's all my fault."

Something inside Patsy was screaming, but she managed to keep her voice calm. Her hysterics would only make Mrs. Walden more nervous. "Is Wendy all right, Mrs. Walden?"

"She's at the hospital."

"Hospital?" Patsy screamed, her calmness vanquished by a picture of Wendy lying alone in a hospital bed. "Which hospital, Mrs. Walden?"

"It's all my fault."

"Dammit, Mrs. Walden. Is she at Grove City Medical?"

"The emergency room."

"Oh, my God," Patsy said, wondering if Kenny knew, and if he did, how he was handling it. "Is Mr. Sanders there, Mrs. Walden?"

"He's with Wendy. I told him I'd call you."

Patsy dropped the phone and rushed out of the office, not even taking the time to lock her door. Kenny needed her. Wendy needed her. She had to get to her family.

Chapter Fifteen

Kenny forced a smile on his face for Wendy's sake, but inside he was screaming. He'd never get over the horror he'd experienced when he'd seen her fall. One minute she'd been waving merrily at him, and the next she'd been barreling to the ground. It had all happened so quickly. He'd known she was going to fall, but he'd been powerless to do anything but shout her name across the school yard.

"Ouch," Wendy said, and Kenny immediately focused his attention on the small, beautiful child sitting on the emergency-room table. "You're squeezing my hand too hard, Daddy."

He loosened his hold on her hand and wished again that Patsy were here. He needed her. "I'm sorry, Peanut," he said. "We don't want you to have a cast on each arm, now do we?"

Wendy's eyes lit up. "I've never seen anybody with two casts before. Daddy—"

"No," he said firmly. "You can't have two casts." He wouldn't be able to look at this one cast without seeing her fall again and experiencing that moment when he'd thought she was dead.

"Where's Mama Patsy?" Wendy asked.

Kenny wondered the same thing. He wanted her here. He needed her here. "She'll come in a little while. Mrs. Walden called her for us."

"Can we stop for ice cream on the way home?" Wendy asked.

Kenny glanced at the intern, who smiled at Wendy's question. "Of course. And you can have as much as you want."

"Can I really?"

Kenny nodded. At this point, he could deny her nothing. Every little girl was entitled to eat too much ice cream once in a while, he rationalized.

He looked toward the door and wondered again where Patsy was.

Patsy didn't bother looking for a parking space. She saw a spot in the No Parking zone near the emergency-room entrance, but out of the way of the ambulances, and quickly pulled into it.

Once inside, she rushed up to the first nurse she saw. "I'm Mrs. Sanders. My daughter, Wendy, was brought in here. How is she? Where is she?"

The nurse placed her hand on Patsy's shoulder and gave her a comforting pat. "Wendy's fine. She only fractured her arm. Mr. Sanders and the doctor are in with her now." She pointed to the back of the room. "Go through those double doors. Wendy's in the second room on the right.''

Patsy thanked the nurse and rushed through the double doors, needing to see for herself that her little girl was okay. She stopped outside the cubicle and took a deep breath.

"Mama Patsy," Wendy yelled, when Patsy appeared in the doorway. "We've been waiting for you. What took you so long? See my cast?''

"Keep your arm still, Wendy," Kenny and the doctor said in unison when she attempted to lift her arm for Patsy to see.

Patsy smiled at the frown that crossed Wendy's face at their rebuke. That frown told Patsy that Wendy was basically fine. "You aren't giving your daddy and the doctor any trouble, are you?''

Wendy shook her head. "No, ma'am.'' She looked up at Kenny. "You're hurting my hand, Daddy.''

Kenny gave a fake chuckle that Patsy knew was for Wendy's sake, then looked over at her with anguished eyes. "Why don't we let Mama Patsy hold your hand for a while?'' he said.

Patsy's heart contracted at the pain she saw in Kenny's eyes. She wanted to pull him into her arms and reassure him that Wendy was fine, but she knew by the way he stepped back when she moved to take Wendy's hand that he was doing all he could not to lose it in front of his daughter.

When she took Wendy's small hand in hers, all her fears about the accident returned. She and Kenny could have lost this precious bundle. She rubbed her eyes with her free hand to keep Wendy from seeing the tears that had so quickly formed.

"You got something in your eye, Mama Patsy?" Wendy asked.

Kenny stepped up next to her and placed a comforting arm around her waist. She rewarded him with a quick glance of thanks, and his eyes told her the touching comforted him, too.

"I'm fine, Wendy," Patsy said, relaxing against Kenny's strong arm. "Now which one of you is going to tell me what happened?"

"I fell off the jungle gym at school," Wendy said matter-of-factly. "I was scared at first, then Daddy said I was a big girl and I wasn't scared anymore."

"You *are* a big girl," Patsy said, then glanced at Kenny. His face had gone blank and his eyes had a horror-filled glint to them.

"And then Daddy drove us to the hospital. We were going so fast. I've never been that fast, have I, Daddy? And I wasn't scared, either. It was like being on a roller coaster. Except my arm hurt."

"You've been a brave girl, Wendy. I'm proud of you."

Wendy grinned. "Daddy says we can stop for ice cream on the way home and I can have as much as I want."

"Of course you can. A big, brave girl like you deserves to have all the ice cream she can eat." Patsy looked back at Kenny, and the tension that lined his face pained her. "Kenny, the doctor is almost finished here. Why don't you go get a cup of coffee?" she suggested, hoping he'd use the time to relax and take care of himself. "Wendy and I'll be okay until you get back."

"You're sure?" he asked, then looked from her to Wendy. When they both nodded, he headed for the door. "I'll be right back."

"Don't rush," Patsy called after him. "Wendy and I need to have some girl talk anyway, don't we, Wendy?"

The little girl giggled, and Kenny closed the door.

He was back in ten minutes. "It doesn't take long to get a cup of coffee," he said at Patsy's lifted brow.

She wished he'd taken more time for himself, but she knew it was useless to try and get him to leave again, so she turned her attention back to Wendy. "Will you let me be the first to sign your cast when the doctor's finished?"

"Sure," she said, then sheepishly looked up at her father.

"I thought you said I could sign it first," he reminded her.

"Well..." Wendy began. Then her eyes lit up. "You can sign at the same time. Then you both can be first. Do we have two pencils?"

Kenny laughed, and this time Patsy was sure it was a real laugh. "Peanut, one day you're going to be the best lawyer on the planet." He looked down at Patsy. "She has the art of compromise down pat."

"Do you want to be an attorney when you grow up, Wendy?" Patsy asked.

The child shrugged her small shoulders. "I don't know. I think I want to be a hairdresser."

"A hairdresser?" she and Kenny asked at the same time. Patsy recovered first. "Why do you think you want to be a hairdresser, sweetheart?"

"If I was a hairdresser I could cut my own hair," she said promptly.

Patsy and Kenny laughed again, and the three of them settled into relaxed chatter while the doctor finished applying Wendy's cast.

When he was almost done, Wendy asked, "Where's Mrs. Walden? Didn't she come with us, Daddy?"

"She sure did, Peanut, but I haven't seen her since we've been here." He looked at Patsy. "Did you see her when you came in?"

"I haven't seen her," Patsy said, remembering how upset the older woman had been. Though earlier she'd been pretty irritated with Mrs. Walden, now she wanted to thank her. "Maybe she's in the cafeteria. Where did you get your coffee?" she asked Kenny.

"A vending machine near the waiting room."

"I want to see her. She rode in the car with me and Daddy," the little girl explained to Patsy.

Patsy released the child's hand, then patted her uninjured arm. "I'm sure she wants to see you, too, sweetheart." Patsy turned to Kenny and spoke in a hushed tone. "She was pretty upset when she called me. I'd feel better if I went and looked for her."

Kenny nodded, moving quickly to take Wendy's hand in his again.

"You'll bring her to see me, won't you? She can be first to sign my cast, too."

Patsy looked down at her daughter. "Of course," she said. Not wanting to leave the room, she brushed her hand across Wendy's forehead.

"Go ahead," Kenny urged. "I'd like to personally thank Mrs. Walden myself."

Patsy dropped her hand from Wendy's forehead and slowly moved toward the door, still not wanting to leave them.

"Don't hold my hand so tight this time, Daddy," Patsy heard Wendy say as the door closed behind her.

Patsy spotted Mrs. Walden as soon as she made it through the concession line with her juice and sandwich.

The older woman sat at a corner table with her head bowed, staring into what looked like a cup of coffee. Patsy straightened her shoulders and headed for the table.

"Mrs. Walden," she said, and the older woman raised tear-stained brown eyes to her. "Is it all right if I join you?"

The other woman nodded, then stared back down at her cup.

"Wendy's fine, Mrs. Walden," Patsy said after she was seated. "It's just a fracture. She wants you to be one of the first people to sign her cast. You'll do that for her, won't you?"

"It's all my fault," Mrs. Walden said.

Patsy placed a hand atop Mrs. Walden's folded ones on the table. "It's nobody's fault. Children have accidents. Nobody blames you. And you shouldn't blame yourself."

"If only..." The older woman stopped when her voice broke.

"Don't do this, Mrs. Walden. Everything's fine. Wendy wants you to come visit her. And so does her father."

"He does?" Mrs. Walden raised wide, questioning eyes, and again Patsy felt a familiarity with the older woman.

She squeezed her fingers. "Of course he does. He wants to thank you for being so helpful. And I want to thank you for calling me like you did."

"But she could have died, and it would have been all my fault."

A piercing pain grabbed Patsy's heart at the thought

of Wendy dying. "She could have," she said calmly. "But she didn't. She's fine. And she's happy."

"You don't understand," the older woman insisted, removing her hands from the table and placing them in her lap.

Patsy began to think she really didn't understand. After all, she hadn't been there. And Kenny and Wendy hadn't really given her any details. But she knew Kenny wouldn't be thanking Mrs. Walden if the accident had been her fault. "Why don't you tell me what happened?" Patsy said, hoping that talking would help the older woman.

"The children were playing on the playground while they waited for their parents." Mrs. Walden fidgeted with a paper napkin, practically tearing it to shreds. "Wendy was on the jungle gym." A slight smile formed around the woman's mouth, and Patsy noticed for the first time that she had dimples.

"She loves the jungle gym. Always races to be the first one on it. That's what she did today. She raced to the jungle gym and started climbing to the top, giggling and laughing all the way. She's such a happy child." Mrs. Walden's smile faded. "She saw her father coming toward her and began waving and yelling, 'Look at me, Daddy, look at me.' Oh, God," Mrs. Walden said, then began to cry uncontrollably.

Patsy got out of her chair and knelt next to Mrs. Walden, thinking the woman needed a good cry.

"I turned for less than a second," she was saying, "to sneak a look at him. I only wanted to look at him."

Patsy wondered why Mrs. Walden felt she had to *sneak* a look at Kenny. The older woman couldn't have a crush on him, could she? "It's all right, Mrs. Walden. Really it is. Wendy's fine."

"But I almost killed her," she said again. "I almost killed my own granddaughter."

Patsy knew she'd misheard Mrs. Walden, so she asked, "Granddaughter?"

"I turned for a split second to look at him and she fell. I saw the anguish in his eyes and heard his loud cry, but it was too late. When I turned back to Wendy, she was already falling, and I knew I couldn't catch her."

Patsy held Mrs. Walden while she cried what Patsy thought was going to be an endless stream of tears. She was glad when the woman's sniffles finally began to subside. She wanted to understand what Mrs. Walden had meant when she'd called Wendy her granddaughter. Maybe it was something simple, like Wendy calling her Aunt Patsy when she really wasn't her aunt. That could be it, but Patsy felt it was something more. Much, much more.

"Oh, dear," Mrs. Walden said, trying to dry her eyes with her shredded napkin before giving up and getting a fresh one from the holder in front of her. "What must you think of me, crying like this? I assure you I'm much more composed in front of the children."

Patsy smiled, then moved back to her chair. "I'd probably be crying now myself, but I'm not sure I'd be able to stop if I started." She knew she and Kenny had to wait until Wendy was home and safely asleep in her own bed before they could give in to their tattered emotions.

"Well," Mrs. Walden said. She attempted to pick up her cup, but her hands trembled so much that she gave up. "I hope you don't take the ramblings of a sobbing old woman too seriously."

"Mrs. Walden," Patsy said slowly, "why did you call Wendy your granddaughter?"

The older woman found a sudden interest in the silver salt and pepper shakers. "It's nothing. I refer to all the kids as my grandchildren. I'll admit, though, that Wendy is my favorite."

Patsy didn't believe her. She decided to take it from another angle. "Why did you feel you had to *sneak* a look at Kenny?"

Mrs. Walden smiled, but Patsy didn't believe joy was its cause. "Now you've gone and embarrassed me, Mrs. Sanders. Even old women like me appreciate good-looking men."

Patsy knew the older woman was lying, but she couldn't understand why. What was she hiding? Patsy stared at her, trying to remember where she'd met her before. She was sure she had. While she studied the older woman's full face, Mrs. Walden smiled again, and Patsy's eyes locked in on her dimples. The older woman said something, but Patsy didn't hear her. She now knew what was familiar about her. It was her smile. Her dimples. Just like Kenny's. Just like Wendy's.

It couldn't be. It couldn't be! Could it?

"Is everything all right?" the woman asked.

"Mrs. Walden, did you know that Kenny was adopted?"

Her eyes answered that question and the one Patsy hadn't asked.

"You're his mother, aren't you?"

The older woman sighed, then shook her head slowly. "I'm not his mother. His mother died three years ago."

"I don't believe you. You *are* his mother."

Tears formed in her eyes. "I'm the woman who gave

birth to him," she stated simply, "but she was his mother."

Patsy slumped back in her chair as if someone had punched her in the face. "You're really his mother?"

She nodded. "In all the ways that don't count. I'm his *biological* mother. Like I said, she was his real mother."

A thousand questions whirled in Patsy's mind, but most important to her was the safety and happiness of her new family. "Why are you here?"

Mrs. Walden leaned back in chair, and for the first time, Patsy thought she looked tired, old, defeated. "I wanted to see him."

"Are you saying you moved to Grove City because Kenny is here?"

"I had to see him and know that he'd had a happy life. Can you understand that?"

Though Mrs. Walden's eyes pleaded that she understand, Patsy wasn't ready to be accommodating yet. "You didn't have to move here to do that. How did you know he was here, anyway? I thought those records were sealed."

"They are sealed."

"So how did you get the information?"

"I can't answer that, Mrs. Sanders. It would get some very nice people in trouble and I won't do that."

"So you *stole* the information," Patsy said accusingly. "And then you came spying on him."

Mrs. Walden leaned forward in her chair. "I wasn't spying on him. I needed to know he was happy. You're a woman, a mother—surely you can understand that."

Patsy's anger left her as quickly as air leaves a popped balloon. She did understand. "When are you going to tell Kenny who you are?"

"I'm not."

"If you don't, I will," she stated, knowing she couldn't be a party to the woman's lie. "He deserves to know."

"Does he deserve to have his life disrupted? Does Wendy?"

Patsy's answer to both questions was no. Kenny and Wendy deserved a stable, peaceful life, but she couldn't keep this information from him. "You should've thought about that before you came here. What were you thinking, getting a job at Wendy's school and in her class?" Fear began to bubble up in Patsy. What Mrs. Walden had done was much like what a stalker did. What if the woman were unbalanced?

"I'd never hurt them," Mrs. Walden said in answer to Patsy's unasked questions. "And I'm not crazy."

A part of Patsy believed her, but who knew what lurked in people's minds? "Why should I believe you?"

The woman sat back in her chair and seemed to consider Patsy's words. "I've been in Grove City for over a year now. I've been Wendy's teacher since the beginning of the term. If I'd wanted to hurt them, I could have already done it."

"When are you going to tell Kenny?" Patsy asked again.

"I'll tell him when the time is right."

"That's not good enough."

"I can't tell him now, Mrs. Sanders," she pleaded. "I don't think I'll ever forget the look on his face when he saw Wendy fall. You would have thought she was falling from a high-rise and not from a jungle gym. But he thought she was going to die. I saw it in his eyes. He believed it, Patsy." Mrs. Walden began shaking her head. "I don't think he's ready for another emotional shock so soon after that, do you?"

Patsy agreed with the older woman. Kenny needed some time to get over Wendy's fall and subsequent fractured arm. The little girl was his life. He'd lost so much, she could imagine how he must have felt when he'd thought he'd lost Wendy, too. She ached to get back to them both.

"You won't tell him, will you?" Mrs. Walden asked.

"No, I won't tell him. At least, not now. But you'll have to tell him soon or I will."

Mrs. Walden nodded. "I know."

Patsy stared down at her tray and realized she hadn't taken one bite of her sandwich. She had too much on her mind to eat.

"Do you think he'll hate me?" the older woman asked softly, her voice full of uncertainty.

"I honestly don't know what his initial response will be," Patsy answered. "But I don't think he'll hate you."

"I wouldn't blame him if he did. He's probably wondering what kind of woman would give up her child."

Patsy felt Mrs. Walden's pain, but had no words of comfort to offer her.

"When did they tell him he was adopted? How long has he known? Why hasn't he tried to contact me?"

The rapid-fire questions reminded Patsy of Wendy, and she smiled. "His parents never told him he was adopted. He found the adoption papers a few years ago, after they'd been killed in a car accident."

"Oh, no," Mrs. Walden said. "That must have been too much for him to deal with then. I wish they'd told him. It's not right that he had to find out that way."

Patsy felt the older woman's concern and love for

Kenny. "He's pretty strong, Mrs. Walden. He handled it."

The older woman didn't look so sure. "But he didn't try to find me."

"How do you know he didn't?" Patsy said, feeling her sadness and not wanting to add to it. At least, not right now.

Mrs. Walden lifted sorrow-filled eyes to Patsy. "I have my name and address listed in the registry. One phone call and he would have found me."

Chapter Sixteen

Patsy closed the book and stopped pretending she'd been reading. After going for ice cream, she and Kenny had brought an exhausted Wendy home and put her straight to bed. How quickly and quietly she'd gone to sleep showed how tired the child was. Patsy and Kenny had sat at her bedside long after she was asleep, reassuring themselves that she was okay.

Patsy had tried to convince Kenny to come to bed with her, but he'd declined. Her heart ached for him. She could imagine the nightmares he was reliving. And he still had to deal with Mrs. Walden. His mother. Patsy covered her face with her hands.

When she saw Kenny, Wendy and Mrs. Walden together in the hospital room, she'd wondered why she hadn't made the connection before. The family resemblance was undeniable. If you knew what to look for, that is. Patsy was sure no one else would make the connection.

She stopped her musings when Kenny trudged into their bedroom. "Are you going to be all right?" she asked, not liking the tension she saw in his face.

"I'm fine," he said without much conviction. "You okay?"

"I'm fine and so is Wendy. A lot of kids get fractures."

"We didn't."

"Pure luck, I assure you." She smiled at the memory of their youthful pranks. "We were a lot more reckless than Wendy is."

Kenny slipped off his shirt and dropped down on the end of the bed. Patsy saw the tension in the bunched muscles around his neck and shoulders and automatically sought to relieve him. She waddled on her knees to the end of the bed and placed her hands on his shoulders. "You've got to relax," she said, then began working her fingers into his muscles. "Wendy's fine."

Kenny dropped his head to give her better access, but he didn't say anything. Patsy directed all her energy into the massage. If this was the only thing she could do for him, she planned to do her best.

She noticed the shaking in his shoulders before she heard his soft sobs. "Oh, Kenny," she said softly. "My poor, sweet Kenny." She lowered her hands from his shoulders and wrapped them around his torso, resting her face on his back. "Wendy's fine," she murmured, stroking her hands across his chest.

"You didn't see her fall, Patsy. I've never been so scared in all my life. I could have lost her."

"But you didn't. And you won't. Not for a long time."

For a short moment, his hands covered the ones that stroked his chest, then he cleared his throat. "Look, I'm fine. Why don't you get some sleep?" He stood up and looked down at her. "Thank you," he said simply, then turned on his long legs and went into the bathroom.

Patsy stared at the door separating them, missing the comfort of his body against hers. Her plan had been to comfort him, but she now knew they had comforted each other. Just like a husband and wife should.

When he returned to the bed a little while later, showered and dressed in his standard pajamas, she turned to him. "Do you want to talk about it?"

"Not tonight. Maybe tomorrow."

That was okay with her. She knew he needed time. She didn't want to talk, either, but she needed something, some connection with him. She wanted the closeness they'd shared before he'd gone into the bathroom.

"I'm sorry about your celebration," he said. "I promise I'll make it up to you."

Patsy appreciated his concern, but it wasn't necessary. "Don't even think about it. Anyway, we did celebrate."

He looked over at her, a question in his eyes. "I know I was a bit out of it, but I think I'd remember a celebration."

She smiled, her heart going out to him. "We had ice cream, remember? All the ice cream we wanted."

She would have paid millions for the laugh her words coaxed out of him.

"You're good for me, you know that? I don't know what I would have done without you today." He laughed again, in a self-deprecating way that made Pasty wince. "Probably broken Wendy's hand."

"You looked like you were doing okay when I got to the hospital."

She thought she saw him grin. "I put on a good show. I couldn't let Wendy see how nervous I was. The doctor either, for that matter. He would've put me in the bed next to her."

Patsy inched toward him and placed her hand on his arm. "Don't be so hard on yourself. Wendy's fine."

He laid his other hand on top of hers. "I wonder how many times you've told me that today. Tell me a few hundred more and maybe, just maybe, I'll believe it." He paused. "You know what I want to do right now?"

Patsy shook her head, wondering if he felt the need to hold her as she felt the need to hold him.

"Go back to her room and make sure she's okay."

The apprehension in his eyes made her heart turn over. She loved this man with all her heart and she was grateful for the life they had in front of them. Very grateful. "Why don't we go together?" she suggested. "I could do with a look at her myself."

They got out of bed and went to Wendy's room together. Kenny opened the door and they peeked in. The light from the hallway illuminated the sleeping child's face. "You want to go in?" Patsy asked in a whisper.

Kenny shook his head. "She's fine. I don't want to wake her."

Patsy nodded. They stood looking at Wendy for a few minutes longer, then Kenny closed the door quietly, dropped an arm around Patsy's shoulder and escorted her back to their bedroom.

Keeping his arm around her shoulder, he turned so he could look down in her face. "I meant it, you know. I'm glad you were with me today. It didn't really feel right until you got there."

Her insides churned with sudden hopefulness and she smiled. "Glad to be of service."

Kenny lowered his head and did what he'd wanted to do ever since she'd walked into the hospital room. He kissed her. The kiss started soft, but quickly became hard and demanding. He needed this. He needed her. Not to satisfy some physical hunger, but to satisfy an emotional need deep in his soul. It was as if kissing her, touching her, made the world real and safe for him. He wanted to keep kissing her. He wanted to do more than kiss her. He lifted his head and pulled her into his arms.

"Am I holding you too tight?" he asked when she groaned.

"Never," she murmured against his chest.

He contented himself with holding her for a long while. When he moved to release her, she tightened her arms around him.

"Don't," she murmured. "I need you, Kenny."

Kenny's heartbeat hammered in his chest. Her words could mean a million different things. What *did* they mean? he wondered.

"Kenny," she murmured softly, "will you kiss me again?"

He stared down at the face he'd come to cherish more than he'd ever thought possible and saw the yearning in her wide, expressive eyes. She hid none of her feelings for him. She wanted a kiss. But she also wanted more. Much, much more.

He lowered his head and pressed his lips against her much softer ones again. She immediately slid her arms around his neck and pulled him closer to her. He groaned against her mouth, then picked her up and carried her the few steps to the bed. With her arms still around him and his mouth covering hers, he gently lowered her to the mattress. He adjusted his body so that all his weight wouldn't be on her and gave himself up to the kiss.

He luxuriated in her soft, but urgent exploration of his mouth. Her hands slid down the front of his pajama top and her fingers slipped open the buttons so she could stroke the hairs on his chest. He moaned in pleasure, trying to keep his desire in check while she worked her magic on him.

His desire escalated as her soft hands traveled slowly down his stomach to his navel, which was partially covered by the waistband of his pajama bottoms. Unable to hold himself back any longer, he covered her breasts with his hands, feeling their softness beneath her flannel gown. Her muffled groan was his reward.

She pulled away from him, and her passion-glazed eyes held his. He didn't know what she was looking for in his eyes, but he hoped she found it.

"Are you sure you want to do this, Patsy?" he asked, knowing that if she stopped now he'd die of unfulfilled desire.

Keeping her eyes glued to his, she slipped open the clear buttons of her navy gown, then pulled the garment over her head and threw it onto the floor behind her.

His eyes took in the full length of her, admiring the black lace of her bra and panties, which contrasted so with her now-discarded flannel gown. Had she worn sexy lingerie like this every night? he wondered as his eyes zeroed in on her full breasts, straining at the edges of her bra. He couldn't stop his fingers from tracing a line around the top of the flimsy undergarment. When his hand covered her breast and squeezed lightly, Patsy sucked in her breath.

His eyes shot back to hers. "You like that?"

Her teasing tongue traced her full lips, causing him to pull her against him and press his mouth against hers again. His hands went behind her and in short order un-hooked her bra.

He leaned away from her and she hunched her shoulders, causing her bra to slide down her arms. He pulled the bothersome garment away from her and threw it over his shoulder onto the floor.

She giggled. "In a hurry?"

"No way," he was able to say before he rolled onto his back and pulled her atop him. His hands caressed her from her cute, little ears to her supple thighs, remembering every touch that made her shiver.

He sucked in his breath when she pushed his pajama top off his shoulders. He shrugged out of the garment and threw it on the floor. Next, her hands slid down his chest to the snaps on his pajama bottoms. "Kenny," he heard her murmur in frustration. "I can't get it open."

She lifted her lower body slightly and he reached between them and fumbled with his snaps, all the while recognizing that the only thing separating his hands from the center of her passion was the thin film of her black lace panties.

He took advantage of his good fortune and cupped her in his hands briefly before pushing his pajama bottoms and briefs down his legs and kicking them off. When he was naked, he rolled her onto her back so he could have better access to her breasts. She moaned in pleasure when he took the taut nipple of one of her firm mounds in his mouth while his hand caressed the other.

Patsy lifted her hips to press closer to him, aching for the release she knew he'd give her. Her tongue slipped out of her mouth in pleasure as he suckled at her breast. He released her nipple, then brushed his lips across its stiff tip. His lips trailed a path from the peak of her breast to her shoulder and on to her armpit. When he kissed her there, her lower body lifted off the bed in spasm.

The more Kenny pleasured her, the weaker she felt and the more frustrated. Frustrated because she wanted to touch him as he was touching her, but she couldn't. He zapped her energy with his every kiss, his every touch.

"Kenny," she murmured, but forgot what she was going to say when he slipped a hand inside her panties. Instead, she groaned as one of his fingers eased inside her, giving her a preview of what she could expect from him.

"You're so wet," he said, and continued his exploration of her.

She twisted frantically against him, her heart slamming against her ribs. She felt bereft when he removed his finger, but not for long, for he reached around and snatched the thin lace material away from her.

She pressed her lower body to his, needing his heat to satisfy her. She felt him hard and long, and she wanted him.

She ran her hands down between their bodies and touched him, tentatively at first, but then more boldly as his moans of pleasure grew louder.

He shifted slightly, giving her better access to that part of him that sparked her curiosity and drove her passion. Her eyes widened when she saw him.

"We'll fit perfectly," he said, and she shut her eyes, embarrassed that he'd read the question in them.

He kissed her eyelids while positioning his body over hers. "Look at me, Patsy. I want to see your eyes when I come inside you."

She opened her eyes, unable to resist him, and was

rewarded with one of his full-blown smiles, dimples and all.

"Now that's better," he said, pressing his knee against her leg but not taking his eyes from hers.

She opened for him, anxious to feel him inside her.

"You're so beautiful," he whispered, his mouth dragging kisses down her jaw.

She wanted to tell him he was beautiful, too, but she couldn't form the words. Her brain seemed focused on one thing only—the imminent joining of their bodies.

She gasped when he passed her entrance, then purred with pleasure as he sank deep within her. She watched the play of emotions across his face while he waited for her body to become accustomed to his. Perspiration beaded on his forehead, and the realization that he exercised great restraint made her grow warmer, if that were possible.

She lifted her hips against him and he responded with a thrust of his own. His lips parted and he increased his pace. For a split second she wondered if the rocking sound made by the bed would waken Wendy, but that thought was soon forgotten as he took her mouth in his and his tongue teased hers in a rhythm that matched his other loving movements.

Patsy met him thrust for thrust until she reached a place she'd never visited before. Her fingernails dug into his back and pulled him tighter against her. Her whole body grew still, then the tidal wave of her release flooded over her.

Kenny felt the tension build in Patsy's body, then saw her eyes widen in surprise and pleasure when she reached the pinnacle of her excitement. The joy and pleasure her release gave him brought him over the top immediately. With a final thrust, he emptied himself into her.

Kenny woke with Patsy sprawled over him, her soft snoring as sexy as hell. He'd have to tease her about it. He hadn't noticed her snoring in all the nights they'd slept together, so either he'd made a good showing tonight or he'd bored her senseless. He grinned, knowing he definitely hadn't bored her.

As he gazed on her beautiful, naked form, his body heated with renewed desire and he wanted her again. He considered waking her, but the peaceful expression on her warm face stopped him. He could wait, he told himself, then closed his eyes.

Five minutes later, he was still awake and he still wanted her. He'd either have to get out of bed or go ahead and make love to her. He chose what he thought was the nobler of the two options. He got out of bed, slipped on the pajama bottoms he'd discarded earlier, then padded out of the room to check on Wendy once more.

When he peeked into his daughter's room this time, he could smile. She was fine. And she'd continue to be fine; he felt sure of that now. He closed the door silently and made his way downstairs.

He went directly to the closet in the family room and pulled out the brown storage box that held videotapes. He didn't know why he wanted to look at them now, when he hadn't in two years, but he did.

He slipped a tape in the VCR, not bothering to see which one it was, then eased back on the couch to watch it. His face and Wendy's were the first images he saw. They were asleep on the couch, the two-year-old Wendy resting on his chest.

"Wake up, sleepyheads," Leah's voice called from off camera.

Kenny remembered the lazy Saturday all those years ago when Leah had caught him and Wendy on tape. She'd been bad about sneaking up on them and taping them when they weren't looking. He remembered those times with a poignant gladness.

Leah's smiling face appeared on the screen next. Kenny remembered how he'd taken the camera and forced her to pose with Wendy. Had she been happy then? he wondered. He pressed the Pause button on the remote control and stared into the face of the woman he'd loved for so much of his life.

Why hadn't he realized how unhappy she was? Why hadn't she told him? *She did tell you,* he reminded himself.

Then she should have made me understand how unhappy she was, he argued. They were married. She should have told him, given him some signal. She shouldn't have gone to that lawyer behind his back. That was betrayal.

He looked again at the happy, loving face on the screen in front of him and wondered what had driven her to do something so deceitful. Had she been that unhappy with him? Had he been that insensitive to her feelings?

Kenny admitted they'd argued more than once about his working hours, but he'd explained to her that as the new guy in the district attorney's office, he had to distinguish himself. He had to work hard now in order for them to have a secure future. She hadn't understood at first, he knew. She'd complained that she and Wendy missed him and needed him. She'd told him he was missing some of the most important days in Wendy's life. His answer had been to buy her a video recorder so she could capture those moments for him. He shook his head at the arrogant ignorance he'd displayed.

Leah's complaining soon stopped, and he had assumed she finally understood what he was trying to accomplish with the long hours at the office. Obviously, she hadn't. He had the letter from her lawyer to prove it.

He wondered if Leah knew he had found out about the attorney. He'd never been able to confront her with it. At first he'd been too hurt to even discuss it. Then he'd become angry. By the time he'd reached a point where he could talk about it, the doctors had told them about Leah's illness and its prognosis. There was no use bringing it up then.

Kenny wondered what his life would have been like if Leah hadn't gotten sick. Would she have divorced him and taken Wendy with her? Or would they have worked through their problems? He'd never know the real answer, but he didn't think the latter would have happened. Leah had reached her limit if she'd consulted an attorney.

Had he really treated Leah that badly? he wondered. He thought he had, and for that he was ashamed. So ashamed he hadn't even told Leah about reading the letter about the divorce. So ashamed he hadn't told Patsy about it, either.

Patsy. He knew she deserved the truth. He should have told her before they were married. She deserved to know he'd failed at his first marriage and might fail at this one. But he hadn't wanted her to know, hadn't wanted her to question whether he'd make a good husband. She'd married him thinking his and Leah's marriage had been perfect, and he'd done nothing to let her know the reality.

You're a phony, Kenny Sanders, he said to himself. A great big liar. You ended one marriage with a lie. And you've started the second one with a lie.

His thoughts turned to Patsy and the night they'd just shared. That hadn't been a lie. He'd made love to his wife, the woman who was right now enjoying a peaceful and contented sleep after consummating their marriage. Patsy would never betray him the way Leah had. That's why he loved her. That's why he was *in love* with her.

''I'm in love with Patsy,'' he said aloud. ''I'm in love with Patsy.'' The words rolled around in his mind until he was sure of them. He *was* in love with Patsy. He didn't know when it had happened, but he'd fallen in love with her.

An overwhelming joy filled him and he wanted to rush upstairs and share his revelation with her. But he couldn't. How could he tell Patsy he loved her before he told her how he had failed Leah?

He looked back at Leah's smiling face on the screen in front of him. He'd always thought he was angry with Leah because she'd betrayed him, but now he wondered. Had he been in love with Patsy, on some level, even when he was married to Leah? And had that love kept him from seeing and responding to Leah's needs?

As he sat in the silence of the family room with Leah's face smiling out at him from the television screen, a voice in his mind kept asking, ''Was Leah the one betrayed?''

Chapter Seventeen

Patsy missed the warmth of Kenny's body as soon as he got up from the bed. Still full of the wonderful experience they'd shared, she rolled over into the space he'd vacated and immediately went back to sleep.

She became concerned when she awoke again sometime later and found Kenny still wasn't in bed. She got up, slipped her robe on over her naked body, which still tingled from his touch, and made her way to Wendy's room. She quietly eased the child's door open, expecting to see Kenny seated beside his daughter's bed. Instead, all she saw was Wendy, resting comfortably. Patsy pulled the door closed and went downstairs, following the stream of light coming from the family room. What was Kenny doing down here so late? she wondered.

She saw him sitting on the couch, his eyes focused on the TV, the remote-control device in his hand. A rush of insecurity invaded her at the thought that he preferred the television to spending the rest of the night in bed with her.

"Is something wrong, Kenny?" she asked cautiously.

He looked over at her, staring as if he didn't know who she was. Recognition flashed quickly, but not quickly enough. "Nothing's wrong," he stated without emotion.

"What are you doing?"

"Nothing," he said, then flicked the remote control. But not before Patsy saw a freeze-frame of Leah's face on the screen.

She hated the distance she felt between them now. It was as if the time they'd spent in each other's arms a few hours ago had never happened. "Why are you down here?" she asked. If she had felt secure, she would have added, "I missed you," but she didn't.

Kenny turned his attention back to the TV, even though the sound was muted. "I'm fine. I needed to be alone for a while."

"Oh," she said, his words like cold water splashed in her face. What had she expected? That after making love to her, he would pledge his undying love and never leave her side? She knew better than that. She was in love with Kenny, but he'd expressed no such feelings for her. She knew he was still in love with Leah.

Patsy's knees went weak when understanding dawned. Kenny felt guilty about making love to her when he still loved Leah and felt married to her. Patsy backed away toward the door, her sudden realization like a band around her chest, cutting off her air supply. "I guess I'll leave you alone then."

Kenny looked up at her, and the pain in his eyes only served to further rip her heart apart. "Thanks," he said briefly.

She turned and slowly climbed the stairs to their bed-room. She'd known Kenny and Leah had shared a special love, but the magnitude of the pain she'd seen in his eyes tonight surprised her. She wondered what it would be like to have a man love her the way Kenny loved Leah. The way he *still* loved her.

Patsy slipped off her robe and lifted the sheet so she could slide back into bed. When she remembered her naked state, she grabbed the gown she'd discarded earlier and slipped it over her head. She turned back the covers to look for the panties she'd worn, the vivid memory of Kenny's strong fingers ripping them from her body burning in her mind.

She found the torn panties on Kenny's side of the bed and her bra on the floor. She put the bra in the hamper and the panties in the bathroom wastebasket, then climbed onto her side of the bed and tried to go back to sleep and forget the horrors of the night.

Kenny hadn't come to bed all night. That was Patsy's first thought when she woke up the next morning and found he wasn't in bed with her. She quickly dressed and peeked in on Wendy before going downstairs to make breakfast. She deliberately avoided the family room. If Kenny needed to be alone, she'd leave him alone.

The understanding she'd felt when she left him sitting in the family room last night was long gone, replaced by anger. Anger at herself for confusing the fantasy of having Kenny be in love with her with the reality that he was still in love with Leah. Anger at herself for expecting Kenny's feelings for her to change because hers for him had changed. Fool, fool, fool, she thought.

She managed to make breakfast without interruption.

Neither Kenny nor Wendy had appeared by the time she finished, so she ate a quiet meal alone. Afterward, she put her plate in the dishwasher and placed Kenny's and Wendy's meals in the oven. He could heat them up when he got up.

Patsy checked in on Wendy once more before leaving for work. She told herself that Kenny could stay home with the child today and she could go to work. She and Kenny needed the time apart, anyway. But as she looked at Wendy, she knew she couldn't stand being away from her all day. No, she'd come too close to losing her.

As she closed the door of the little girl's room, Patsy decided she would spend the morning in her office while Kenny stayed with Wendy, then she'd come home so Kenny could get some work done.

When she got back downstairs, Kenny was coming out of the family room, a folded blanket in his arms. "Good morning," she said, the awkwardness of last night still between them.

Kenny cast a guilty glance at the blanket in his arms before looking up at her. "Patsy, about last night—"

"Don't, Kenny," she said, not wanting to hear him say he was still in love with Leah. "There's no need to say anything. We comforted each other last night. We both knew it wouldn't have happened if we hadn't been so upset about Wendy," she lied, knowing that before Wendy's accident she had planned to sleep with Kenny.

"Comforted each other?" he asked, with a sarcasm she didn't understand. "Is that what we were doing? Comforting each other?"

She inclined her head toward the blanket in his hand. "If it had been something more, don't you think you would have spent the night in bed with me instead of alone on the couch?"

Kenny opened his mouth, but no words came out. Patsy took advantage of the moment. "Look, if it's all right with you, I'll go into the office this morning while you stay with Wendy. I'll come home around lunchtime so you can get some work done. Is that okay with you?"

He nodded. "It works."

She nodded, too. What else could she do? "Well, I guess I'd better get going."

"I guess you'd better," she heard him say as she picked up her briefcase from the foyer table and headed out the front door.

Patsy surprised herself by making it all the way to her office without giving in to the despair that dogged her. She'd known when she married Kenny that he was in love with Leah. It was nothing new. What was new was that Patsy had fallen in love with her best friend, her husband. And she'd slept with him and experienced the passion she hadn't wanted to feel again. So much for a safe, platonic marriage, she thought wryly. There was nothing safe or passionless about her feelings for Kenny.

Around ten o'clock, after resolving problems for two customers, Patsy called home to check on Wendy. The little girl answered the phone.

"Hi, Mama Patsy. You didn't eat breakfast."

Patsy smiled and her heart filled with joy and happiness. She'd married Kenny because of Wendy. She'd stay married to him for the same reason. "Yes, I did. You were asleep."

"Why didn't you wake me up? Daddy woke me."

Patsy had figured as much. "How are you feeling, sweetheart?"

"My cast got wet but Daddy dried it off."

Patsy could imagine Wendy getting the cast wet and a lot worse.

"Can I go to school tomorrow?" the child asked. "I want all the kids to see my cast. Mrs. Walden said she'd tell them about it, remember?"

Patsy had forgotten, but now she remembered. She also recalled, though she hadn't really forgotten, that Mrs. Walden was Kenny's mother and Wendy's grandmother. Patsy would have to speak with the older woman soon, to make sure she still planned to tell Kenny who she was. "We'll have to see how you're feeling before we decide about school tomorrow. But even if you can't go then, we can invite some of your friends over to sign your cast. Would you like that?"

"Yippee," Wendy said, then yelled, "Daddy, Mama Patsy says I can have a party tomorrow."

"Wendy," Patsy called, but it was no use. The little girl was still talking to her father.

Kenny's voice came on the line. "What's this about a party?" he asked.

"Not a party. Wendy got a bit overexcited. I told her that if she didn't go to school tomorrow, she could invite some of the kids over to sign her cast." Patsy couldn't believe she was engaging in this normal conversation when her heart was breaking. "That's all right, isn't it?"

"Of course it's all right. You don't have to get my permission."

Patsy wasn't too sure about that. She'd overstepped her bounds in one area. Maybe she'd overstepped them in another.

"Patsy," Kenny began.

"I have to go," she lied, guessing he still wanted to talk about last night. Well, she didn't. She'd already said what she needed to say. And she didn't want to hear him tell her how much he regretted sleeping with her because he still loved Leah. "See you in a couple of hours."

"Okay," he said.

"Okay," she repeated awkwardly, then hung up before he could say anything more.

She stared at the handset and wondered how she would cope with the nagging pain. Here she was, in another relationship gone off track. Except this time she knew why it had done so. It was her fault. She'd fallen in love and expected the rules to change. Too bad—

"How was the celebration?" Marilyn's voice interrupted her thoughts.

Patsy looked up and saw her friend standing in the open doorway. "We didn't celebrate," she said, waving Marilyn into her office. "Wendy broke her arm yesterday and we had to take her to the hospital."

"How is she?" Marilyn sat on the windowsill behind Patsy's desk.

"She's fine. She's already lining up people to sign her cast."

"That sounds like Wendy. I'll have to get by to see her, since I missed her party."

"I'm leaving here in a few minutes. Why don't you come with me? We'll make an afternoon of it. After lunch we can sit in the backyard, have some iced tea and do some catching up. It'll be fun."

"I'd love it."

Patsy shared a strained lunch with Kenny, Marilyn and Wendy. If Wendy hadn't been so excited about her new cast, the meal would have been a disaster.

"I have to make a run to the courthouse," Kenny said, wiping his mouth with a paper napkin. Patsy had guessed from the dark suit he wore that he'd be going out.

"Can I come, too?" Wendy asked, her bright eyes

sparkling. The fractured arm hadn't doused any of her energy.

Kenny tugged on one of her braids. "Not today, Peanut. You need your rest."

"But I'm not tired," she said, pouting. "Everybody at the courthouse can see my cast."

Kenny scooted his chair back and took his dishes to the sink. "Not today," he repeated.

"But—" she began.

"No buts, Wendy," he said with finality. He looked at Patsy. "I'll be back around four."

She nodded, then spoke too brightly. "We'll see you then. I hope all goes well in court."

Kenny said his goodbyes to Marilyn and Wendy and left the house. Patsy released a sigh when she heard the front door close.

"Can I get down now?" Wendy asked. "I want to go play with my dolls."

"Sure, sweetheart," Patsy said, smiling at the child.

Wendy scrambled from her chair and ran out of the kitchen.

"What was that all about?" Marilyn asked.

"What?" Patsy responded, though she had a pretty good idea.

"You and Kenny. The tension was so thick in here you could cut it with a knife. What happened? I thought you two were getting along well."

Patsy stood and began clearing the table. "I did, too."

"Then what happened?"

"It's a long story," Patsy said, rinsing the dishes and putting them in the dishwasher.

"I've got all afternoon. Do you want to talk about it?"

Patsy dried her hands with a plaid dish towel. "Let's

have tea on the deck,'' she suggested. She placed a pitcher of tea and two glasses on a serving tray and took them outside.

"So, what's up?" Marilyn asked, when they were seated in facing deck chairs.

Patsy studied her friend's face, not sure where to start.

"Did you two have a fight?"

Patsy shook her head. A fight wouldn't leave the pain she still felt. "Not really. Let's say we had a communication problem."

"And?"

"Kenny and I made love for the first time last night, then Kenny got up and spent the night in the family room looking at videos of him, Leah and Wendy."

"He didn't."

Patsy nodded. "Unfortunately, yes, he did."

"Men," Marilyn said with a huff. "Sometimes they can be so damned insensitive."

Patsy agreed with her friend's assessment, but she also thought Marilyn's indignation was fueled by something a bit more personal. "Are you having man problems, too?"

"Hah. There's no man in my life and there probably won't be for a while. I need a break."

"Come on," Patsy encouraged. "I told you my problem. Now tell me yours. What happened?"

Marilyn rolled her eyes. "Derrick happened."

"I knew it." Patsy snapped her fingers. "I just knew it."

"You couldn't know much because there's not much to know. We only went out one time."

Patsy remembered the tension between Marilyn and Derrick the day they helped her move into Kenny's house. "The night of my wedding?"

"Right. Biggest mistake of my life. That man is a total jerk."

Patsy leaned forward. "Come on. What did he do?"

Marilyn shrugged, then stood. "He didn't *do* anything. It's his attitude. Every time I think about him, I get angry."

"You care about him, don't you?"

"How can you ask that? I just said the man was a jerk."

"Unfortunately, that usually doesn't matter. He wouldn't make you so upset if you didn't care."

Marilyn sat back down. "I did care, but I don't anymore."

"This is me you're talking to, Marilyn. Emotions aren't that easily controlled. You might not want to care, but you do. The question is what are you going to do about it?"

"Nothing. What can I do?"

"Does Derrick know how you feel?"

"I doubt it. He's such a thickheaded man. He's been spoiled by too many women. Looking like Denzel only makes it worse."

"Maybe you're just the woman to unspoil him?"

"No woman can change a man," Marilyn said quickly. "If he changes, it's because he wants to."

Patsy considered the truth in her friend's words. "Maybe you're right," she said.

Marilyn placed a comforting hand on Patsy's knee. "It's different for you and Kenny. You've made a commitment to each other. You can work through your problems."

"It's not a problem. It's a reality that I have to face and deal with."

"Maybe Kenny's just putting some old demons to

rest," Marilyn offered. "Give him some time. He'll come around. He cares more for you than either of you realize."

Patsy wished her friend's words were true, but she refused to hold out any hope. She'd come into this marriage with her eyes open, and she would keep them open. She, Kenny and Wendy could still be happy, and they would be. She'd make sure of it. Or she'd die trying.

. . . .

. . . .

. . . .

. . . .

. . . .

. . . .

Chapter Eighteen

Later that night Kenny plodded up the stairs to the bedroom he shared with Patsy, not sure of the reception he'd
get, given the coolness she'd showed him during dinner.
He stopped outside the door, took a deep breath, then
turned the knob. Patsy glanced up from the book she
was reading, nodded, then returned her attention to the
pages in front of her.

Well, he asked himself, what did you expect after the
way you treated her last night? He kicked off his shoes
and cast a quick look at his wife, sitting on the bed in
another of her flannel nightgowns. From the intense way
she stared at the pages, he guessed the book must be a
very interesting one. Hah, he said to himself, it couldn't
be that interesting, since it'd been lying on the headboard since the first night they'd slept together. That
night she had intended to use it a barrier between them,
and apparently, she had the same plan for tonight. He

hadn't let her get away with it then and he knew he shouldn't let her get away with it now.

"Patsy?" he said.

She lifted her eyes from the page and peered over the top of her book. "Yes."

Damn, he thought. She wasn't going to make this easy for him. "About last night..."

Her eyes dropped back to the page. "What about it?"

"I think we should talk about what happened."

She continued to stare down at the book for so long that he thought she was going to ignore him, but finally she closed the volume, settled back against the headboard and folded her arms across her chest. "Okay, talk."

Kenny didn't know how to start, so he sat down on the edge of the bed next to her and toyed with a thread that had come unraveled on the comforter.

"You're not talking," Patsy said, then reached behind her and got her book.

"Interesting story?" he asked.

"Hmm, yes," she said, her attention again riveted on the paperback.

He took it out of her hands.

Her eyes widened and hot flames flashed in them. "What do you think you're doing?"

He handed the book back to her and grinned.

She snatched it out of his hands. "What's so funny?"

He stood and stared down at her, then tapped the cover. "It was upside down."

She looked down at the book, then back up at Kenny, her mouth open. She quickly clamped it shut.

He couldn't help it; he laughed, long and loudly.

Patsy snapped the book closed, then slid down in the bed, pulling the covers up to her chin. "Good night," she shouted, wanting to make sure he heard her over his laughter. Well, she thought, she was glad he found the situation funny. She certainly didn't. Marilyn was right—men could be damned insensitive.

She closed her eyes and hoped he'd move away from the bed. When he didn't, she opened them again and glared at him. "Tell me, Kenny. What's so funny? Are you laughing at the way I threw myself at you last night?"

His laughter stopped immediately, and she read the pain registered in his dark eyes. She'd hurt him and she should be glad, but she wasn't. When he hurt, she hurt.

"You can't think that," he said, his eyes pleading with her to tell him she didn't believe it.

Patsy didn't see any need to hide her real feelings. It was time they had this out. "Why shouldn't I, Kenny? One minute, you're making love to me and the next you're kicking me out of the family room so you can stare at Leah."

"That wasn't the way it was," he declared, but she didn't listen.

"You told me I was bringing Theo and my parents into this bedroom, and I thought about it. I really thought about it, Kenny. I wanted this marriage to work so badly that I wrestled with what you'd said. I examined myself. I examined my feelings for you and my feelings for Theo and my parents. And I concluded you were right. I *had* brought the fears from those relationships into this bedroom and projected my insecurities onto you. Do you know why I came to that conclusion?"

"Because it's the truth?"

She laughed, and the harsh sound seemed to come from some distant planet. "What do you know about truth? Do you remember the day you told me that you hadn't brought Leah in here with us? Was that the truth?''

"She was my wife, Patsy. I loved her."

"Liar," she declared.

Kenny's mind went back to the videotape and the smile on Leah's face. Patsy couldn't know what a disappointment he'd been to Leah, could she? He *had* loved her. Maybe not well, but he'd loved her. "I loved her, dammit. I *did*."

Patsy shook her head slowly. "You don't get it, do you, Kenny? You keep using past tense, but the truth is you're still in love with her. The truth is you were so guilty about making love—" she looked up at him, then corrected, "no, having sex with me that you couldn't bear to spend the night in my bed. You couldn't bear to have me near you." Her voice broke. "How could you be so cruel?"

He reached for her, but she scooted away. "Don't touch me," she said. "Don't get me wrong. I'm not upset because you still love her. I knew that coming into this marriage, and I could deal with it. I'm upset and disappointed that you lied to me."

"I didn't lie to you," he declared.

"Yes, you did. You told me she wasn't in here. You told me that and then you made me think it was my problem. How dare you do that to me? How dare you?"

He reached for her again. "Patsy..."

Patsy brushed her hands across her eyes, hating the weakness that her tears represented. "If you hadn't been thinking so much about sex, everything would have worked itself out. But no, your hormones got so out of control that you started saying things you didn't mean." She shook her head again. "I expected more from you, Kenny. So much more."

Kenny shoved his hands in his pockets, as if he knew any further attempt to touch her would be rebuffed. "It's not like that. You know it's not like that. I didn't lie to you."

"Right, Kenny," Patsy sneered. "Then explain to me why you spent the night in the den. Explain to me why you practically kicked me out when I came down to see about you. Explain that to me."

"It's not that easy," Kenny said, wanting to explain the feelings he had for her, but not trusting that he understood them himself. Last night he'd learned he was in love with her, but now, looking at her and seeing what he'd done to her with his callousness, he wasn't sure he knew what being in love was. Maybe Patsy was noting the same weakness in him that Leah had. Maybe she would—

"Forget it, Kenny. Let's forget all of it. Let's chalk last night up to both of us needing comfort and let it go at that. We got married to provide a home for Wendy. We can do that."

"And our marriage?" he asked.

She shrugged. "We'll pretend last night didn't happen. We'll go back to where we were before last night."

He nodded agreement, not seeing he had any other choice.

"But Kenny," she warned, "you're going to have to deal with your feelings for Leah. I'm not saying you have to stop loving her, but you have to find room for both of us in your heart if you want that real marriage you've been talking about. I won't make love with you again until I'm sure your guilt won't make you walk away from me. I won't do it."

"I'm sorry, Patsy," he said. And he was. He was sorry he hadn't been honest with her in the beginning about the problems in his marriage to Leah. Patsy was his best friend. She would have helped him unravel his feelings. She would have helped him find perspective and balance. But he hadn't shared his shameful secret with her.

Now he wanted to share it with her. All of it. He wanted to tell her how lost and alone he'd felt when he'd found out about Leah's talk with the divorce attorney. He wanted to tell her how disappointed he'd been in Leah and in himself. He wanted to tell Patsy that he had made love to her last night because he was *in love* with her. He wanted to tell her how guilty he felt for falling in love with her so quickly and so completely when he'd loved Leah so poorly. He wanted to tell Patsy that he was afraid he had always loved her and that his love for her had been the reason he'd failed Leah.

He wanted her to help him fit together the pieces of the puzzle that would put in perspective his love for Leah and his love for her. But it was too late. She was no longer his best friend. She was his wife. And she didn't trust him.

"Daddy." Wendy pulled on the sleeve of her father's shirt. "You're not listening to me," she complained.

Kenny forced his gaze away from Patsy's back. How could she stand there and cook breakfast like nothing was wrong? he wondered. He looked down at Wendy, whose lips were turned down in a slight frown. "I'm sorry, Peanut. What did you say?"

"How come you're looking at Mama Patsy like that?" his daughter asked in a way that only she could.

He knew Patsy had turned around, but he didn't look up at her. "Is that what you were saying?" Kenny asked, praying that for once his daughter would be distracted from her question.

The child gave an exaggerated sigh. "Mrs. Walden, Daddy. Mrs. Walden let me sit in the front seat of the bus yesterday when we went to the museum. I looked down on the road and everything."

"You did? And what did you see?" Kenny asked, thankful to Mrs. Walden for providing alternative breakfast conversation.

Wendy scrunched up her nose. "Stuff."

"Stuff. What stuff?"

Wendy grinned. "Stuff stuff."

"Stuff stuff or stuff stuff stuff?" Kenny asked, joining in the game.

Wendy laughed. "Stuff stuff stuff stuff."

"You're sure it wasn't stuff stuff stuff stuff stuff?"

Wendy held up five fingers. "It was stuff, stuff, stuff, stuff, stuff," she said, folding down a finger every time she said the word. "And stuff." She lifted a finger on her other hand.

"Are you sure it wasn't—"

"Breakfast's ready," Patsy said, turning around and placing a platter of biscuits and sausage on the table along with a small bowl of grits. "Will you get the jam out of the refrigerator, Kenny?"

"I'll get it, Mama Patsy," Wendy said, hopping down out of her chair. Kenny watched her open the refrigerator with her left hand and pull out the jam, the cast in no way preventing her from accomplishing the task.

The little girl ran back to the table. "Here it is."

Patsy smiled at the child. "Thank you, sweetheart," she said, then brushed her hand across Wendy's cheek. "You're such a good girl."

Kenny wished Patsy would brush her hand down *his*

cheek. If she did, he'd take her hand in his and pull her into his arms for the kiss he so desperately wanted to give her. Then she'd probably slap his face, he thought wryly.

Things had certainly gotten out of control since the night a week ago when they'd made love. He couldn't get the night out of his mind, while Patsy seemed to have forgotten it altogether. He felt a constant need to touch her, while she seemed to think he'd gotten a contagious case of the plague or something.

"Mama Patsy," he heard Wendy complain. "Daddy's not listening again."

"I am so listening," he said. He was listening. To his heart but not to the breakfast conversation.

"Are you finished, sweetheart?" Patsy asked. When Wendy nodded, she suggested, "Why don't you go get your books? We'll meet you at the door."

Wendy looked from her father to Patsy, then mumbled, "Okay." She scrambled down from the table and ran off in the direction of the stairs and her room.

When Patsy was sure Wendy was out of earshot, she said, "What's on your mind this morning, Kenny? You've been distracted for the past few days and now Wendy's noticing it."

You're on my mind, he said to himself. How much I love you. And I much I want you to love me. And how much I don't want to feel guilty anymore. That's what's on my mind. "Nothing important," he said.

She lifted her coffee cup to her lips and drank the remaining hot liquid. "It must be important or you'd be paying more attention to your daughter."

"Are you criticizing my handling of *my* child?" he asked, more in reaction to his frustration than in reaction to her words, and immediately regretted it.

Patsy slowly set her coffee cup on the table and slid her chair back. She stood up and stared down at him. "You'd better get yourself together, Kenny. She's my child, too. She became my child the day I married you. And I resent your trying to make me feel like an interloper. What's wrong with you these days, anyway?"

"I'm ready," Wendy called from the foyer, and Kenny was granted a reprieve from answering the question.

"I'm coming, sweetheart," Patsy said, then pushed her chair to the table, shot Kenny another glare, grabbed Wendy's lunch box and rushed to the foyer. By the time Kenny arrived, she'd opened the door.

"Don't I get a kiss goodbye, Peanut?" Kenny asked.

He leaned down and embraced Wendy in a big hug. To make up for his inattention at breakfast, he gave her a strong squeeze.

Wendy twisted out of his arms and rushed out the door to the car.

Patsy moved to follow after her, but Kenny grabbed her arm. "Don't I get a kiss, Mrs. Sanders?" He didn't wait for her answer, but leaned his head down to hers and dropped a chaste kiss on her inviting lips, not missing the surprise in her eyes. This was the first kiss they'd shared since the night they made love. The night of their argument.

"What was that for?" she asked when he removed his lips from hers.

He shrugged, then gave her a weak smile. "Nothing."

"Nothing?"

"Nothing."

"I don't understand you, Kenny Sanders," she said, then rushed out the door after Wendy.

Kenny stood in the doorway after the two females in

his life had gone, wondering how a man could have everything he loved within his grasp and still be unhappy. He stepped back and pushed the door closed, then made his way to his office, thankful that his work gave him a reason to stop thinking about his problems.

"I've got it, Carolyn," Patsy called to her secretary. She'd given the young woman a report to prepare and she didn't want her disturbed. "Instructional Technologies," she said into the phone.

"Mrs. Sanders, this is Mrs. Walden from Wendy's school," the older woman said.

"Is everything all right with Wendy?" Patsy asked, fear building in her stomach.

"That's what I'm calling about. She's been a little quiet lately. Not as happy as she usually is. I hope everything is all right at home."

No, everything is not all right at home, Patsy said to herself. And poor Wendy is taking the brunt of it. "Have you spoken with Kenny about this, Mrs. Walden?"

"N-no," the older woman stammered, "I thought I'd talk to you."

"And I think you should talk to Kenny. About Wendy and about what you need to tell him."

"But dear, I don't think it's the right time."

"At the rate you're going, there'll never be a right time. You have to tell him. Kenny's going through a lot right now and he needs to know."

"But if he's going through a lot," the older woman reasoned, "why should I add to his burden?"

Patsy sighed. "Because Kenny's not a child, Mrs. Walden. He's a grown man. And he's a strong man. He can handle it. What he can't handle is more secrets. You have to tell him and you have to tell him now."

"Will you give me a couple of days?" the older woman pleaded.

Patsy turned her chair toward the window and looked out at the bright, sunny day. "I know you're scared, Mrs. Walden. I'm scared, too. I'm frightened for Kenny and you. And for me and Wendy. But we have to get all this out in the open. For all our sakes."

"You're right, dear. And I knew it would come to this. But I never realized how scared I would be. What if he hates me?"

Patsy knew the older woman wanted reassurance, but she didn't have any to give her. "In all honesty, Mrs. Walden, I have no idea how Kenny will respond. He doesn't seem to be handling his emotions very well these days, but maybe this news will be the thing that allows him to finally let go."

"But he's already suffered so much."

"And he's going to continue to suffer until he deals with his pain. He can't keep ignoring it." Patsy spoke of the pain he still felt from Leah's death. Kenny had to deal with his grief and move forward. If he didn't, they'd all be lost. She was sure of it.

"You really think I should tell him?"

"I do."

"Will you be there?"

Patsy wanted to be, but she knew Kenny had to do this alone. "This is between you and him. I'll stay home with your granddaughter."

Patsy heard the older woman sigh. "You know, I've yearned for this day and I've dreaded it. I want him to know. I want Wendy to know. And I want them to love me. Is that wrong?"

Patsy's heart filled with compassion for the older woman. She definitely knew what it meant to want someone's love and not be sure you'd ever have it. "There's nothing wrong with wanting their love. But," she added, "you have to be prepared to love them even if they aren't able to love you back right now."

Mrs. Walden was quiet for a while, then she said, "I'm glad Kenny found you, Patsy. I couldn't have picked a better wife for my son. I don't think I'd be able to tell him this news without knowing he had someone like you at his side to support him."

How Patsy wished Mrs. Walden's words were true. But she wasn't sure they were. For the first time in her life she didn't know where her relationship with Kenny stood. She was still in love with him, but they'd lost each other. She prayed they'd find their way back together soon.

"I'll tell him when he comes to pick up Wendy," the older woman said, drawing Patsy back to the present.

"That's a good idea. I'll meet him at the school and bring Wendy home so the two of you can talk alone."

"Thank you again, Patsy. For everything. For loving Kenny. For loving Wendy. And for keeping an old woman's secret."

Chapter Nineteen

Kenny saw Patsy and Wendy as soon as he drove up to the school. He parked his truck at the curb and ran over to them. He stooped down and hugged his daughter, then looked up at Patsy, with Wendy still in his arms. "What are you doing here? Is something wrong?"

Patsy shook her head. "I thought Wendy and I needed a Girls Out afternoon."

"We're going for ice cream," Wendy explained. Apparently, she thought a Girls Out afternoon was a wonderful idea.

Kenny released Wendy, tugged on one of her braids and stood up. "Why didn't you call me?" he asked Patsy, still not sure everything was all right.

"Mrs. Walden wants to talk to you," she said softly.

"About what?" Now he was sure something was wrong.

Patsy placed her hand on his arm. "Trust me. Everything's fine. Mrs. Walden just has a few things to discuss with you.''

"Why aren't you coming with me? You're Wendy's mother.''

Her smile tugged at his heart, and she surprised him by placing a soft kiss on his lips. "Thank you,'' she said, then looked down at Wendy. "Ready, sweetheart?'' Wendy bobbed her head and Patsy reached for her hand.

"You can't come, Daddy,'' Wendy said. "But we'll bring you some ice cream.''

Kenny smiled and tapped a finger on his daughter's nose. "I'll be waiting for it.''

He watched the two of them walk off hand in hand toward Patsy's car. When they'd driven out of the parking lot, he entered the school for his talk with Mrs. Walden. He found her erasing the chalkboard in Wendy's classroom.

"Mrs. Walden?'' he said. When she turned, he continued, "You wanted to talk to me about something?''

"Why, yes, Mr. Sanders,'' the older woman said, then dropped her eraser.

Kenny raced to pick it up. As he handed it to her, he grinned and said, "Old habits die hard.''

The older woman laughed, and he thought again that she looked very familiar to him. She was a handsome woman, with a complexion similar to his, her gray hair only a little bit longer than his own. She looked about Mrs. Mae's age or a little older and she dressed fashionably. He turned those thoughts off and focused on the reason he was here. "So what did you want to talk to me about?''

"Why don't we sit, Mr. Sanders?'' she said, pointing to the yellow child's table in the corner.

Kenny ambled over and sat in one of the small chairs, his long legs stretched far out in front of him. He took comfort in the fact that Mrs. Walden looked about as comfortable in her chair as he did in his. Again, the sense of familiarity struck him. "Are you sure we haven't met before?" he asked. "I'd swear I know you from somewhere. Do you have any relatives in Grove City?" He wondered if he was picking up on a family resemblance.

The older woman looked down at her hands. "As a matter of fact I do. That's what I wanted to talk to you about."

Kenny relaxed. "So this is a legal problem you're having?" Legal problems he could handle.

"In a way," the older woman hedged.

Kenny leaned forward and covered her hands with his. It was part of his job to make people comfortable enough with him to discuss their personal problems. "Why don't you just tell me? Whatever you say will be held in strictest confidence." He glanced up at the open door. "Do you want me to close the door?"

The older woman nodded. "That might be a good idea."

Kenny squeezed her hand in a gesture of comfort, then got up and closed the door. After he was seated, he covered her hand with his again. "Just start at the beginning and tell me."

"I don't know how to say this," she said.

"Don't worry," he answered with a concerned smile. "You can tell me anything."

"You're sure?"

"I'm sure. You helped me and Patsy the day Wendy fell off the jungle gym. I'm more than happy to help you now. As a matter of fact, I'm honored."

The older woman gave him a smile and Kenny noticed she had dimples. And she reminded him of somebody. He just couldn't place the person.

"It's about my son," she said, interrupting his curious thoughts.

Kenny didn't say anything, having learned from experience that once a client started talking it was best to let her continue at her own pace. He hoped her son wasn't in serious trouble. She was a nice woman and deserved to have children she could be proud of.

"He doesn't know," she continued. "But I have to tell him."

Kenny hoped the older woman didn't have an illness that she'd kept from her son. He hated to think of her being sick.

"My son is..." she began, but stopped.

When she remained silent, Kenny squeezed her hand again. "It's all right. Your son is...?"

"He's adopted," the older woman said.

Kenny's breath quickened in his throat. "Does he know?"

The older woman nodded her head.

"How old is he, Mrs. Walden?" he asked, thinking her son must be about his age and observing that by not telling him sooner Mrs. Walden had made the same mistake as his parents.

"He's thirty-two."

Kenny wanted to laugh at the irony. The guy was *exactly* his age. Maybe they could form a club. "Why haven't you told him?"

She shrugged. "The time hasn't been right. Until now."

"So where do I fit in, Mrs. Walden? This isn't a legal matter. Are you telling me because you heard I was adopted and didn't learn about it until I was an adult? Do you want me to talk to your son?''

The older woman shook her head rapidly. ''You don't understand.''

''I think I do, Mrs. Walden. You're worried about keeping the secret so long. I know. And yes, you should have told him before now, but since you haven't, you need to do it as soon as possible.'' He patted the older woman's hands and gave her the encouragement he thought she was looking for. ''He'll understand. Maybe not at first, but he'll understand.''

The older woman covered her face with her hands and began to sob. ''You don't understand. I've made a mess of things.''

Kenny wished the older woman would stop crying. ''I'll go with you to talk with him, if you like,'' he offered, hoping that would help calm her. ''Tell me his name. Maybe I know him. He lives here in Grove City, doesn't he?''

Mrs. Walden dropped her hands from her face and took both of Kenny's in hers. ''Stop and listen to me. I'm not the adoptive mother. I'm the biological mother. My son doesn't know I'm his mother.''

Kenny's stomach clenched at her words and his eyes met hers. Whose mother was she? he wondered as he studied her face. Her lips were a tight line now and the dimples were hidden. He wished she'd smile again because that's when the familiarity was strongest.

''Oh,'' he said. ''I guess I did misunderstand. But I still don't know what you want me to do. How can I help? Do I know your son?''

She nodded. ''Very well.''

''Who is he, Mrs. Walden?'' Kenny asked, anxious to

know the answer and relieve the tension that had settled around him.

"Kenny," she began, and his eyes widened because that was the first time she'd called him by his first name.

Then he knew. And he wondered why he hadn't guessed it before now. He removed his hand from hers. To her credit, she didn't take her eyes from his.

"I'm your mother," she said with more calm than he knew she felt.

"My mother is dead," he almost growled. He could tell by her flinch that his missile had hit its designated target.

"I'm your biological mother," she clarified.

Kenny stared at her. Her dimples were his. And Wendy's. He whispered a curse under a breath.

"I know this comes as a shock to you." Mrs. Walden's words rushed out. "But I am your biological mother."

"What are you doing here?" he asked, not quite believing this gentle old woman had deserted him.

"I moved here after my husband died because I had to know if you were happy."

"Your husband?" he asked, wondering if her husband was his father. His biological father, he corrected. His own dad was dead.

"He wasn't your father," she said in answer to his unasked question. "Your father was killed in a boating accident before you were born. He didn't even know I was pregnant."

His father was dead. Grief for the unknown man burned in his eyes.

Mrs. Walden reached in her purse and handed him a photograph. "You look a lot like him," she said.

Kenny studied the old, faded photograph. He immediately saw his own resemblance to the young man in the picture, and he felt as if a door inside him opened. He felt a connection sure and strong to the person who shared his face. Such a young man, Kenny thought, and how sad he'd died so young. *Before I got to meet him,* he added in his mind. Kenny placed the picture facedown on the table in front of him, not wanting to look at the familiar features any longer.

"I thought I was doing the right thing when I gave you up for adoption. I was young and my parents convinced me it would be unfair to keep you. People weren't as liberal as they are now. They said you'd grow up with the stigma of being a bastard. I didn't want that for my baby. Not when there were so many families who could give you the one thing I couldn't—a name. When I look at you now, I know they were right. Your parents were good to you, weren't they?"

He nodded, but he didn't want to share much of his life with this woman. His mother. His biological mother. The woman who had given him and his daughter their dimples. He wondered if everybody on her side of the family had dimples. "Why are you telling me this now?"

She sat back in her chair. "I wanted you to know that you were loved, not abandoned. I didn't abandon you. I gave you up because I thought it would be best for you and it was."

Abandoned—that was it. That was how he'd felt. Abandoned when his parents had been taken from him in the accident. Abandoned again when he found out they weren't his real parents. Abandoned when he learned about Leah's divorce plans. And abandoned once more when she died and left him alone to raise

Wendy. Everyone who was supposed to love him had abandoned him.

Everyone except Patsy. She'd always been there. And he knew she always would be. He really knew it. Deep in his heart, where it counted, but also in his head. "Why should I believe you didn't abandon me?" he asked, not willing to go down without a fight.

"As soon as it became legal to register with the agency, I left my name and address so that if you ever wanted to get in touch with me, you could. But you never did."

He wanted to tell her how wrong she was about his not wanting to find her, but he couldn't form the words to explain that it was his fear that had prevented him from taking that step. It was easier to live with not knowing than to go through another abandonment.

He stood up abruptly, overtaken by a sudden need for fresh air and time alone to think. "Thank you for telling me, Mrs. Walden."

She looked up at him with tear-filled eyes. "I'm proud of you, Kenny. I know I have no right to be, but I am. You're a good husband with a loving wife and a good father with an adoring and adorable child. You have everything I could have wished for you."

"I have to go," he said. He rushed to the door, but stopped before he opened it. He turned back and looked at his biological mother. Her shoulders shook slightly and he knew she was crying again. The friend in him wanted to offer comfort, but the son in him couldn't. Right now it was all he could do to hold himself together. He closed the door quietly and made his way to his truck.

"I hear his truck driving up now, Mrs. Walden. I have to hang up." Every half hour since she and Wendy had gotten home and found Kenny hadn't yet arrived, Patsy had been trading phone calls with the older woman. Patsy had made the first call, worried that Kenny hadn't taken the news that Mrs. Walden was his mother very well.

"You'll phone me tomorrow and let me know how he is," Mrs. Walden reminded her.

"If Kenny doesn't call, I promise I will. Now stop worrying. He's home and he's safe."

Patsy hung up and rushed to the door. Kenny pushed it open just as she was about to open it for him.

"Where have you been?" she asked, her fear now turning to anger. "You could have called, Kenny. I've been worried sick."

Kenny stared at her. He'd come to a lot of conclusions while driving around, thinking about what he'd learned form Mrs. Walden. "You knew what she was going to tell me, didn't you?"

Patsy stepped back from his penetrating gaze. "Yes, she confided in me."

Kenny strode by her and marched to the kitchen. She followed after him.

"Why didn't you tell me?" he asked, pouring himself a glass of orange juice from the jug in the refrigerator.

"She asked me not to."

Kenny slammed the refrigerator shut. "She asked you not to? What about me? I'm your husband."

"I know who you are. I've always known you are. You're the one who's had a problem with it."

He put the glass to his lips and drank all the juice, then slammed the glass down on the table. "Tell me this, Patsy. What is it with the people I love and secrets?"

The hurt in his voice tore at her heart. "Oh, Kenny," she said and moved to touch him, but he snatched his arm away.

"We're talking about secrets," he reminded her. "Are you keeping anything else from me that I should know about?"

Patsy's head jerked back as if she'd been slapped. "I don't deserve that attitude and I don't deserve that tone. I only found out the night of Wendy's accident and—"

"You knew the night of Wendy's accident?" he yelled.

"Keep your voice down," she warned. "You're going to wake up Wendy."

"You knew the night of Wendy's accident," he said again, this time in a hoarse whisper. "And you didn't tell me?"

"She begged me not to, Kenny."

"Someone who's practically a stranger begged you not to tell your husband and you went along with the stranger?" he asked incredulously.

"She's not a stranger and you know it. I'm not going to let you make me feel guilty about this. I swear I'm not."

Kenny dropped down onto one of the kitchen chairs. "God forbid you should feel guilty."

His sarcasm wasn't lost on her. "Look," she said, "I'm going to bed. When you get ready to talk, I'll talk, but not like this."

"Answer me one question, Patsy?" he asked as she turned to walk out the door.

She glanced back at him. "What?"

"Did you sleep with me that night because you felt sorry for me? Was it a pity—"

Whack! Patsy reached across the table and slapped his

face before the ugly word came out of his mouth. "How dare you, Kenny Sanders? How dare you try to sully what we shared? I loved you that night, dammit. I still love you. I'm *in love* with you, you idiot." Patsy planted her hand across her mouth after the words she'd held in her heart for so long rushed out, but it was too late. She turned quickly and raced up the stairs to the bedroom.

She wanted to slam the door, but decided against it when she remembered the sleeping Wendy. Instead she closed the door and leaned against it, her eyes shut. "Kenny Sanders is the biggest jerk in the world," she said aloud.

The phone rang and she pushed away from the door to answer it before the sound woke Wendy. The ringing stopped before she reached the nightstand, and she assumed Kenny had gotten it. She waited for a couple of seconds to see if the call was for her. When Kenny didn't come get her, she kicked off her shoes and headed for the bathroom, hoping a nice warm bath would calm her down.

After reassuring Mrs. Walden that he was fine, and surprising himself by inviting her to Sunday brunch with him, Patsy and Wendy, Kenny ended their telephone conversation and rushed upstairs to Patsy. She was in love with him and that was all that mattered. What a relief he'd felt when she'd thrown the words at him. Not exactly the way he wanted to hear the news, but he'd take what he could get.

Mrs. Walden's declaration that she hadn't abandoned him had opened the floodgates to the guilt and pain he'd felt over the last few years. During the long drive he'd taken after meeting with her, he'd grieved as he hadn't been able to do. But he knew it was his last stop that made the difference. He'd visited the cemetery and forgiven Leah and his parents for the hurt they'd unknowingly caused him. Then he said goodbye to them and sped home to begin his life with Patsy.

He counted his blessings every time he thought about Patsy and the patience and love she'd shown him, though he doubted she knew that from the way he'd behaved when he'd entered the front door. It was his fault, he admitted. It hadn't occurred to him until he was running up the sidewalk to the house that Patsy must have known what Mrs. Walden was going to tell him. Her "Girls Out" afternoon with Wendy had been staged. That discovery had been fresh in his mind when he met her at the door; thus the fiasco.

But he'd been wrong to think Patsy's secrecy put her in the same category as Leah and his parents. If Mrs. Walden hadn't told him her secret, he didn't doubt that Patsy would have. He knew her well enough to know that.

He shook his head and his lips turned up in a secure smile when he reached their bedroom door. His marriage to Patsy would never be dull, he was sure of that. He'd told her once to always tell him what she thought. Well, she'd taken him at his word. And he would always love her for that.

"Fool, fool, fool," she was saying to herself when he opened the door.

"If you're a fool, I'm a fool," Kenny said softly.

She turned and saw him standing in the doorway, a lazy grin across his face, and she knew she'd love him until the day she died.

"I'm in love with you, too," he said, moving with long strides in her direction.

Her face crumbled. She could handle almost anything,

but she couldn't handle this. "Don't, Kenny. Don't lie to me. I married you knowing how you felt about Leah. I can live with that, but I can't live with you pretending you have feelings for me that you don't have."

Kenny looked at her standing proudly in front of him, her fists clutched to her sides, her eyes flashing, and he knew he would always love her. She was his heart. His dark angel. And he'd almost lost her.

He'd loved Leah as best he could, and his friendship with Patsy had never come between them. He knew that now. He'd loved Patsy for most of his life, but he hadn't fallen in love with her until that day at the ice-cream shop when she'd used her coach analogy to help Wendy understand how they were going to work together as parents. There was no reason that loving Patsy should make him feel guilty about the problems in his marriage to Leah. He just thanked God for giving him a second chance, and he thanked Leah for teaching him how to make the second time around so much better than the first.

With his feelings about the past finally resolved, there was nothing standing between him and Patsy, and that was exactly the way he wanted it. He wanted her in his arms with nothing between them and he wanted her there now.

He reached for her, and when she started to push away from him, he held her close and wouldn't let her go. "Look at me," he said.

She tilted her strong, adversarial chin up and looked at him.

"I'm *in love* with you," he whispered.

Patsy felt as if her bones were melting. Those were the words she wanted to hear, but she only wanted them if they were true. "Why did you turn away from me that night, Kenny?'' she asked, hating the hurt in her voice but needing to understand how an experience that had been so beautiful for her had caused him nothing but guilt and shame.

"Because I was a fool," he said, pulling her tighter against him. "I knew that night that I was in love with you, but I didn't know how to handle the feelings."

She eased her head back from him and looked up into his eyes. "But—"

"No buts," he said, pressing a finger to her lips. "Tonight we're going to do something tonight that we haven't done in a long time."

She struggled to get away from him. "Oh, no, we're not," she said.

Happiness and love for Patsy, Wendy and the family they'd have together filled him, causing a wide grin to spread across his face. "We're going to do that, too, but later. After we talk."

"Talk?" she asked with suspicion.

"Yes, talk. I'm going to tell you everything I've been wanting to tell you and you're going to tell me again that you're in love with me. You think you can handle that?"

His words coupled with his gorgeous, dimpled smile and his sincere, yet passionate eyes sent shivers of shock, bands of comfort and gallons of hope flooding through her. "I can handle it," she said. And she knew she would gladly spend the rest of her life telling him how much she loved him.

"Say it again," Kenny asked. He and Patsy sat cuddled in each other's arms on the family-room couch. They'd been this way since he'd told her all his secrets and she'd told him all hers. Now, they were sharing the intimate words all lovers share.

"You're going to get tired of hearing it," Patsy said. "I've told you a hundred times already."

Kenny squeezed her shoulders. "Tell me again. I need to hear it."

"I'm in love with you, Kenny Sanders," Patsy said, gazing up in his face so he could read the truth in her eyes.

"One more time," he coaxed.

"Kenny..."

"Okay, I'll settle for that." He pressed his lips to hers. "You say my name like you want me."

"I do," she murmured.

"Enough to marry me again?"

Her eyes widened. "What?"

Kenny moved away from her and slid to the floor on one knee. "Will you marry me, Patsy Morgan?" he asked with all the passion he felt for her.

She felt the love in his words and knew life couldn't get any better than this. "My name is Patsy Sanders and I'm already married to you. I don't need another ceremony, Kenny. I meant the things I said at the first one."

Kenny squeezed her hand. "I meant them, too, but our first wedding was incomplete."

"What do you mean by that?"

"We had a real wedding, but we did not by any means have a real honeymoon. And I want one. A real one. Now I'm asking you again, and this time I want the right answer. Will you marry me?"

She grinned, her heart full of love for the man who'd been her friend for as long as she could remember and who was now her husband. "We don't have to get remarried to have a honeymoon. And as soon as you get off your knees and take me to bed, I'll show you."

Though he was tempted by her offer, he shook his head. "Not good enough. I want you all to myself on some secluded beach. I want to make love to you over and over and over to make up for every day of this marriage that I've wanted you, but couldn't have you. I want to show you in every way possible how much I love you."

"Oh, Kenny..." she began, but stopped because of the tears that flooded her eyes. She didn't know what she'd done to deserve this kind of love, but she was grateful, so grateful, that she had it.

"And there's something else I want from you."

"What?" she asked through her tears, knowing she couldn't deny him anything.

"A baby. A brother or sister for Wendy. Will you have my baby, Patsy?"

"Oh, Kenny," she said again, unable to form the words to express how much she loved him and how much she wanted to have his baby. She'd almost given up the dream of having children. And now, more than two years later, she had one child and was making plans for another.

Confident in her love and the life they'd share, Kenny wiped the tears from her cheeks with his thumb, then grinned up at her. "I guess that's a yes."

* * * * *

TRACI ON THE SPOT   BY TRACI

1

Morgan Brigham slowly set down his coffee cup on the kitchen table and stared at the comic strip in the center of his paper. It was nestled in among approximately twenty others that were spread out across two pages. But this was the only one he made a point of reading faithfully each morning at breakfast.

This was the only one that mirrored *her* life.

He read each panel twice, as if he couldn't trust his own eyes. But he could. It was there, in black and white.

Morgan folded the paper slowly, thoughtfully, his mind not on his task. So Traci was getting engaged.

The realization gnawed at the lining of his stomach. He hadn't a clue as to why.

He had even less of a clue why he did what he did next.

Abandoning his coffee, now cool, and the newspaper, and ignoring the fact that this was going to make him late for the office, Morgan went to get a sheet of stationery from the den.

He didn't have much time.

Traci Richardson stared at the last frame she had just drawn. Debating, she glanced at the creature sprawled out on the kitchen floor.

"What do you think, Jeremiah? Too blunt?"

The dog, part bloodhound, part mutt, idly looked up from his rawhide bone at the sound of his name. Jeremiah gave her a look she felt free to interpret as ambivalent.

"Fine help you are. What if Daniel actually reads this and puts two and two together?"

Not that there was all that much chance that the man who had proposed to her, the very prosperous and busy Dr. Daniel Thane, would actually see the comic strip she drew for a living. Not unless the strip was taped to a bicuspid he was examining. Lately Daniel had gotten so busy he'd stopped reading anything but the morning headlines of the *Times*.

Still, you never knew. "I don't want to hurt his feelings," Traci continued, using Jeremiah as a sounding board. "It's just that Traci is overwhelmed by Donald's proposal and, see, she thinks the ring is going to swallow her up." To prove her point, Traci held up the drawing for the dog to view.

This time, he didn't even bother to lift his head.

Traci stared moodily at the small velvet box on the kitchen counter. It had sat there since Daniel had asked her to marry him last Sunday. Even if Daniel never read her comic strip, he was going to suspect something eventually. The very fact that she hadn't grabbed the ring from his hand and slid it onto her finger should have told him that she had doubts about their union.

Traci sighed. Daniel was a catch by any definition. So what was her problem? She kept waiting to be struck by that sunny ray of happiness. Daniel said he wanted to take care of her, to fulfill her every wish. And he was even willing to let her think about it before she gave him her answer.

Guilt nibbled at her. She should be dancing up and down, not wavering like a weather vane in a gale.

Pronouncing the strip completed, she scribbled her signature in the corner of the last frame and then sighed. Another week's work put to bed. She glanced at the pile of mail on the counter. She'd been bringing it in steadily from the mailbox since Monday, but the stack had gotten no farther than her kitchen. Sorting letters seemed the least heinous of all the annoying chores that faced her.

Traci paused as she noted a long envelope. Morgan Brigham. Why would Morgan be writing to her?

Curious, she tore open the envelope and quickly scanned the short note inside.

Dear Traci,
I'm putting the summerhouse up for sale. Thought you might want to come up and see it one more time before it goes up on the block. Or make a bid for it yourself. If memory serves, you once said you wanted to buy it. Either way, let me know. My number's on the card.

Take care,
Morgan

P.S. Got a kick out of *Traci on the Spot* this week.

Traci folded the letter. He read her strip. She hadn't known that. A feeling of pride silently coaxed a smile to her lips. After a beat, though, the rest of his note seeped into her consciousness. He was selling the house.

The summerhouse. A faded white building with brick trim. Suddenly, memories flooded her mind. Long, lazy afternoons that felt as if they would never end.

Morgan.

She looked at the far wall in the family room. There was a large framed photograph of her and Morgan standing before the summerhouse. Traci and Morgan. Morgan and Traci. Back then, it seemed their lives had been permanently intertwined. A bittersweet feeling of loss passed over her.

Traci quickly pulled the telephone over to her on the counter and tapped out the number on the keypad.

*   *   *   *   *

*Look for TRACI ON THE SPOT
by Marie Ferrarella, coming to
Silhouette YOURS TRULY
in March 1997.*

Silhouette®

SPECIAL EDITION™

COMING NEXT MONTH

#1087 ASHLEY'S REBEL—Sherryl Woods
The Bridal Path
That Special Woman!
Forbidden passions sparked to life when ex-model Ashley Wilde reluctantly shared very close quarters with handsome rebel Dillon Ford. Can their turbulent past together allow them a passionate tomorrow?

#1088 WAITING FOR NICK—Nora Roberts
Those Wild Ukrainians
Here is the story readers have been begging for! To Frederica Kimball, it seemed she'd spent her entire childhood waiting for Nick. Now she's all grown up—and the waiting is over!

#1089 THE WRONG MAN...THE RIGHT TIME—Carole Halston
It was love at first sight when virginal Pat Tyler encountered ruggedly handsome Clint Adams. But the ex-marine gallantly pushed the beguiling young woman away. He thought he was the wrong man for her. Could she convince him he was Mr. Right?

#1090 A HERO'S CHILD—Diana Whitney
Parenthood
Hank Flynn died a hero—or so everyone thought. Now he was back to claim his fiancée—and the daughter he never knew he had....

#1091 MARRY ME IN AMARILLO—Celeste Hamilton
Gray Nolan would do anything to stop his baby sister's wedding—even seduce bridal consultant Kathryn Seeger to his side. But this commitment-shy cowboy quickly learned that Kathryn had no intention of changing his sister's mind about marriage, and every intention of changing his....

#1092 SEPARATED SISTERS—Kaitlyn Gorton
Single mom Ariadne Palmer just discovered she has a missing twin sister! Placing her trust in the mysterious man who brought her this compelling news, she must learn what family *really* means....

In February, Silhouette Books is proud
to present the sweeping, sensual new novel
by bestselling author

CAIT LONDON

about her unforgettable family—*The Tallchiefs.*

TALLCHIEF FOR KEEPS

Everyone in Amen Flats, Wyoming, was talking about
Elspeth Tallchief. How she wasn't a thirty-three-year-old
virgin, after all. How she'd been keeping herself warm at
night all these years with a couple of secrets. And now one
of those secrets had walked right into town, sending
everyone into a frenzy. But Elspeth knew he'd come for
the *other* secret....

"Cait London is an irresistible storyteller..."
                                              —*Romantic Times*

Don't miss TALLCHIEF FOR KEEPS by Cait London, available
at your favorite retail outlet in February from

V™ *Silhouette*®

FORTUNE'S Children™

Bestselling Author

CHRISTINE RIMMER

Continues the twelve-book series—FORTUNE'S CHILDREN—
in **February 1997** with Book Eight

WIFE WANTED

The last thing schoolteacher Natalie Fortune wanted was
to fall for her new tenant—sexy, single father Eric Dalton.
The man needed lessons in child rearing! But when an
accident forced her to rely on Eric's help, Natalie found
herself wishing his loving care would last a lifetime.

MEET THE FORTUNES—a family whose legacy is greater than
riches. Because where there's a will...there's a *wedding!*

Look us up on-line at: http://www.romance.net

FC-8

If you're looking for irresistible heroes, the search is over....

Joan Elliott Pickart's

Tux, Bram and Blue Bishop and their pal, Gibson McKinley, are four unforgettable men...on a wife hunt. Discover the women who steal their Texas-size hearts in this enchanting four-book series, which alternates between Silhouette Desire and Special Edition:

In February 1997, fall in love with Tux, Desire's *Man of the Month*, in **TEXAS MOON**, #1051.

In May 1997, Blue meets his match in **TEXAS DAWN**, Special Edition #1100.

In August 1997, don't miss Bram's romance in **TEXAS GLORY**—coming to you from Desire.

And in December 1997, Gib takes more than marriage vows in **TEXAS BABY**, Special Edition's That's My Baby! title.
You won't be able to resist
Joan Elliott Pickart's **TEXAS BABY**.